Praise for Jay Bennett's previous suspense novels

THE SKELETON MAN
"Bennett weaves his story with a deft touch and a high level of suspense that will keep young adult readers turning the page."
—*Los Angeles Times*

SING ME A DEATH SONG
"The rapid-fire dialogue . . . keep[s] the plot moving quickly. . . . [Bennett] maintains the suspense and intrigue at an intense level throughout."
—*School Library Journal*

SKINHEAD
"Powerful . . . [A] page turner."
—*Kirkus Reviews*

COVERUP
"Quick and fun with a satisfying resolution."
—*Voice of Youth Advocacy*

Also by Jay Bennett
Published by Fawcett Books:

THE SKELETON MAN
THE HAUNTED ONE
THE DARK CORRIDOR
SING ME A DEATH SONG
SKINHEAD
COVERUP
THE HOODED MAN

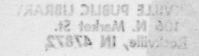

DEATH GRIP

Jay Bennett

FAWCETT JUNIPER • NEW YORK

RLI: $\dfrac{\text{VL 5 \& up}}{\text{IL 6 \& up}}$

A Fawcett Juniper Book
Published by Ballantine Books
Copyright © 1993 by Jay Bennett

All rights reserved under International and Pan-American Copyright Conventions. Published in the United States of America by Ballantine Books, a division of Random House, Inc., of New York, and simultaneously in Canada by Random House of Canada Limited, Toronto.

Library of Congress Catalog Card Number: 93-90206

ISBN 0-449-70423-8

Manufactured in the United States of America

First Edition: October 1993

Chapter

1

I'm caught, he said to himself. Caught in a death grip. And there's nothing I can do about it.

Nothing.

He sat on the plane and looked out the window at the darkening sky and his hand tightened about the violin case that stood on the seat next to him. He always booked an extra seat when he traveled.

For the violin case.

The priceless Guarnerius inside.

He gazed out at the darkening, sullen sky and he remembered the man's words to him.

The voice soft.

So very soft.

Almost a velvet whisper.

The words precise.

Think about it, Shane Lockwood.

Think about it and then do as we want you to do.

All the important critics speak about the brilliant future ahead of you.

1

You've impressed them.

Each and every one of them.

They call you the new prodigy.

Better than Heifetz was in his youth.

Better than Perlman.

Oistrakh.

Think about it.

Think.

The voice became harsh.

But in complete control.

If I chopped off one of your supple fingers, what would happen to your career as a violinist?

One finger.

And you die.

Yes, Shane said to himself bitterly. I would die inside and that would be a worse death than any other.

A death that would stay with me throughout my life.

Never to leave me.

Never.

He sat back in his seat and closed his eyes in pain.

His hand tightened about the violin case.

I'm caught.

Caught.

In a death grip.

Chapter

2

It all began just after the concert in Venice.

That very night.

He saw the Guarnerius put into the hotel vault, the steel door locked shut, and then he turned and walked out of the brightly lit lobby and onto the old cobbled street. The summer night was soft and pleasant and a full moon hung like a giant lantern in a deep and dark blue sky.

Its reflections in the waters of the Grand Canal were golden and glimmering.

A warm, peaceful feeling flowed through him as he walked along the cobblestones and gazed out over the water to the shimmering white buildings on the far shore.

One of the old palaces stood white and ghostly against the night.

Out in midstream a vaporetto glided silently and he watched it until he could see it no more.

A strange sense of loss crept over him.

3

And then it was gone.

He felt tired but satisfied.

It had been a good concert and the audience responded with great warmth and fine appreciation.

All in all it had been a successful trip.

Albert Hall in London, then on to Amsterdam, and now finishing here in Venice.

In a few days he would fly back home.

To a small house he had rented on the outskirts of Princeton.

Shane paused and smiled.

It had been a wise decision to go to the university for his education and use the summer vacations for concerts.

He had also been able to go into New York in the past year to perform at Carnegie Hall and Lincoln Center.

And then a much-acclaimed concert with Muti in Philadelphia.

So it was all working out just fine.

In a sense, he was having his cake and eating it.

He was getting the college education he so desperately wanted and continuing with his career.

Brooke Shields had done it before him at Princeton and made it work.

Yes, she certainly had.

He smiled and thought of the pleasant lunch they had together on campus. She had come back for a visit and then sought him out to give him advice on how to handle the press and other media people during his stay at the university.

"You're becoming a celebrity, Shane. And celebrities are very vulnerable. There are a lot of sharks out there.

4

Waiting to score off you. Always remember that. Take care."

She reached over and touched him gently on the wrist.

"And you're quite handsome. So that can also be a danger."

"Can it?"

"Yes."

And they both laughed.

Now, as he thought of her, he smiled and looked across the gently lapping water to San Giorgio Island shimmering in the distance.

A soft night breeze came up and rippled through his dark brown hair. He put his hand up to smooth the straying hairs back into place and then he stopped for an instant and lowered the hand and looked at it.

The moonlight glimmered over the five separate fingers.

The palm shone gold.

It is gold to me, he thought.

No, more precious than that.

Much more.

And he suddenly remembered the words of the coach of the university football team.

It was just after a concert Shane had given for the athletic fund.

"You're tall and rangy, Shane. Over six feet. And you're strong. You're built like a classic tight end."

"Not like a fiddler?"

"Not at all."

The man paused and grinned.

"How about putting away your violin for a while and coming out for the freshman team? I could use you this season."

And then the man patted him on the shoulder.

"I'll bet if it weren't for your hands, you'd do it."

Shane nodded.

There was a smile in his quiet gray eyes.

"Maybe I would. I've played touch football and liked it a lot. I thought I was pretty good at it. Especially catching long passes."

"But you gave it up."

"I did. My teacher at the time was furious."

"Sorry?"

"Uh-huh."

"Don't be. I was just kidding. Stick to your playing. You're a true champ."

Shane looked up at the glowing Venetian moon and shrugged his broad shoulders.

Maybe I should've been a football player. It would've been great fun.

But it's greater fun doing what I'm doing.

It's more than fun.

It's my life.

Always been that way.

Always.

He began to walk again over the glittering cobble-stones.

Ever since childhood.

And I guess it will be that way till I'm too old to play anymore.

To the very end.

The end.

My eyes will close and the violin will fall away from my dead fingers and shatter into pieces.

Never to be played again.

Never.

A woman came out of the night and stood before him.

He stopped.

"Mr. Lockwood?"

"Yes?"

She was tall, gray haired and well dressed.

"I can't tell you how much I enjoyed your concert tonight."

"Thank you."

She was smiling, but her eyes were dark and piercing.

She spoke again.

Her voice was soft and modulated.

"Particularly the Scarlatti."

"Scarlatti?"

"It's so rarely played. But it's always been one of my favorites. And you were so commanding and yet so delicate with it. Masterful interpretation. Masterful."

He didn't say anything.

He had faltered toward the end of the selection and to him that was the only serious flaw in the entire evening.

He wondered why she had chosen the Scarlatti for praise.

The piece needed more work.

It was a mistake to have scheduled it.

In London, Menuhin had advised him to take it out of the program.

"You're too young for it, Lockwood. Wait till you're older in life and experience. Maybe after a sad love affair. I made the same mistake when I was your age. You'll master it."

But Shane had been stubborn.

7

I guess that's the Irish in me, he thought.

A challenge gets my back up.

My lips clamp together and my hands close into fists.

He heard the woman's voice again.

"Could I have your autograph?"

He hesitated.

"I'd be glad to. But I don't have a pen on me."

"I do."

"Fine."

She opened her large black purse.

The silver clasp shone coldly in the deep night.

"I'm Elaine Stark."

She handed him a black pen and a slip of white paper.

"Stark without the E?"

"Yes."

"I have a distant cousin who spells it with an E. That's why I asked."

"Where does she live?"

"Somewhere in Maine. I believe in Port Clyde."

"Ah, yes. But you live in California. Santa Barbara."

He nodded.

"Yes. My folks are still there. I've gone East for a while."

"For a while. You were born in Santa Barbara and went to school there."

"I did."

"Your father is a noted cardiologist and your mother is an attorney."

"That's true."

"You grew up in comfortable circumstances. It was never a struggle for you."

"I guess I would say that," Shane said and smiled.

"Up to now you've been very fortunate."

"Up to now."

He set the paper against the side of the purse and wrote the woman's name and then signed his own, and as he straightened up to hand the paper to her he saw in the distance, the silent distance, framed against the night, the figure of a man.

Standing stock-still.

Rigid.

Like a dark statue.

Shane could barely make out the pure whiteness of the lean face.

He handed the paper and pen back to the woman.

All the time his eyes were fixed on that still figure.

A faint uneasiness stirred within him.

Through the night stillness he heard her speak to him.

"This was very kind of you, Mr. Lockwood."

He turned back to the woman.

Her dark, piercing eyes were studying him.

"Not at all," he said graciously. "I'm pleased that you liked the concert."

She held the slip of paper up to him.

It gleamed white in the night.

"I shall ever treasure this."

He didn't speak.

Later on, much later on, he would remember those soft-spoken, gentle words with fear and bitterness.

Her dark, probing eyes rested on him for an instant longer and then she turned and walked away.

Her leather heels sounding sharply on the old cobble-stones and then he heard them no more.

But all the while the distant man stood motionless.

9

Shane stared at him.

Then slowly, steadily, the figure stirred and moved back, deeper and deeper into the well of the night.

Until nothing remained.

A sweep of large, heavy clouds suddenly glided over the lambent moon, suddenly and very slowly, blotting it out.

Shane stood alone in the darkness.

Chapter

3

It was during the night that the phone rang.

A sharp, startling sound.

He sat up in bed and then slowly reached over to the night table and picked up the receiver.

It was cold to his touch.

"Yes?"

"Shane Lockwood?"

He didn't answer.

"Is this Shane Lockwood?"

"Yes."

"So it is."

A soft, cultivated voice.

A man's voice.

"So it is. I'm sorry to disturb you at this hour."

Shane looked over to the traveling clock on the night table.

The hands were at two minutes to four.

"But the matter is of grave importance."

Shane waited.

"To you, Mr. Lockwood."

"What do you mean?"

"Your Guarnerius."

Shane felt a chill go through him.

"What about it?"

"Your Guarnerius. That priceless violin. The only one you have played on all these past years."

The man stopped speaking.

Shane's face had become pale.

His hands began to tremble.

Then he heard the voice again.

"It is no longer in the hotel vault."

Shane didn't speak.

"I have it."

"Who are you?"

"That is of no importance to you now."

"Who? Tell me."

"Don't talk. Just listen."

"What do you want with it? What?"

The voice became crisp.

"I believe I told you to listen."

Shane's lips clamped together.

His hands closed into fists.

He waited.

Waited.

Finally he heard the voice again.

"Under no circumstances are you to notify the police."

"What?"

Shane's voice had become a whisper.

"Never go near them."

Shane was now standing in the silent room.

His shadow large against the white wall.

12

The man spoke once more.

"If you even walk within a hundred yards of a police station you will never see your violin again. Do you hear me?"

"Yes."

"Speak to nobody. Do not contact anybody at your hotel. Do not question anybody. I'll know if you did. Have no doubt of that. I will know."

"What do you want with the violin? What?"

"I will tell you in due course."

"Please."

The man didn't answer.

"Money? How much? Tell me."

The man still didn't answer.

"I'll get it for you. But return the violin. Please. I'm lost without it. Completely lost."

"I know you are. That is why I took it."

"You don't have the Guarnerius," Shane said desperately.

"Oh, but I do."

"It's still there. It has to be there."

"I am holding it in my hand now."

"It's in the vault. The steel vault."

He heard the man laugh quietly.

"Money talks its way through steel walls. Money and influence. And I do have both."

Shane was silent.

"You're in Italy now, Mr. Lockwood. An Italy I know much better than you do."

Yes, Shane thought bitterly.

You know it much better than I do.

It's quite evident.

He heard the man speak again.

13

"I will contact you."

"Wait. Please."

But the voice was gone.

There was a click and then complete silence.

Shane stood there, the moonlight sweeping through the open windows and onto his ashen face.

Then he slowly put the receiver down onto its hook.

Slowly.

Ever so slowly.

Chapter

4

He remembered the first time he had ever seen the Guarnerius.

Before even picking it up he knew that this was the violin he had been searching for.

Seeking.

Ever seeking.

And now it was here before his very eyes.

Here, waiting silently, in its black velvet case.

Softly glowing.

Like an ancient, precious jewel.

And he knew.

He knew.

There had been something mystical in the whole search.

He had said to himself, I will know when I see it. I will know then.

And he knew.

Then picking it up out of the case, gently, tenderly, and beginning to play softly, ever so softly.

The warm, secure feel of it.

The touch of his fingers along the instantly familiar strings.

His teacher, a noted violinist, was standing in the afternoon shadows of the room, listening attentively.

A sparkle in his sensitive brown eyes.

"Well, Shane?"

His father, tall and silent, at his side.

Shane continued to play.

Within him a song had started.

A song of serene joy.

As if he had just fallen in love.

A deep and lasting love.

"Well, Shane?"

He slowly lowered the violin and stood looking at them.

He couldn't speak.

There were tears in his gray eyes.

He slowly nodded.

Chapter

5

He sat on the terrace of his suite watching the dawn
come quietly in.

Then the phone rang.

He went back into his room and picked up the receiver.

"Mr. Lockwood?"

"Yes."

"I have your call to Santa Barbara."

"Thank you."

Then he heard his father's steady, crisp voice.

"Shane?"

"Uh-huh."

"You've caught me at the hospital. I'm about to go
into surgery."

"Oh."

"I have three minutes. Make it two. Sorry."

"Sure."

"How was the concert?"

"Fine. Just fine."

"The reviews?"

"Not out yet. Too early in the morning."

"Your mother went to San Francisco. Some women's lib conference."

"How is she?"

"Shane, am I a male chauvinist?"

"What?"

"She said that to me last night. *Me!*"

"Dad, I want to talk to you about something. I . . ." His father cut in.

"Shane, I have to go now. Keep well, Son. We're always proud of you. You know that."

"Yes."

"I'll tell Mom you called. She'll be glad."

"Give her my best."

"I will. Oh, there was an item in one of those supermarket magazines about you and Brooke Shields. Anything to it?"

"We're friends."

"Just friends?"

"That's it, Dad."

"She's a beautiful woman. Quite cultivated."

"I know."

"Shane?"

"Yes?"

"Ah, they're at me again. Listen. There was nothing special you wanted to talk to me about?"

"No, Dad. You'd better go."

"Keep well, Son."

"You too, Dad."

"You're sure there was nothing? . . ."

"I'm sure."

"Good-bye, Shane."

18

Shane put the phone down and went out to the terrace and sat down.

Faint rosy streaks had come into the clear sky, softly staining it.

Below him, in the pool, a girl was swimming, with soft, easy, graceful strokes.

He watched her for a while.

Then suddenly he clenched his hands and got up.

I wanted to talk to him.

I so desperately wanted to.

Now all I can do is wait.

Just wait.

Chapter

6

Within the hour, he heard a soft, persistent knock.

Shane went to the door and opened it.

A short, stout, urbane man stood before him. It was the manager of the hotel.

"Am I disturbing you, Mr. Lockwood?"

"No," Shane said.

"You must forgive me."

The man spoke English fluently but with just a trace of an Italian accent.

He smiled a persuasive smile.

His voice was soft and pleasant.

"My wife was at your concert last night and she wanted me to personally thank you. So I am here to do so."

You're not, Shane thought.

It's something else.

"I'm sorry I couldn't get to the concert but I was busy. Always something to take care of. You understand."

"Yes. I do."

"She wanted me to tell you how much she enjoyed your playing."

"Please thank her for me."

The man bowed slightly.

"I shall."

He turned as if to go, but didn't move from the spot.

"Is everything to your satisfaction?"

"Yes."

"Anything more I can do for you?"

Shane shook his head.

"Oh. Your call to Santa Barbara."

Shane tautened.

"What?"

"Was it clear? No static?"

Shane didn't answer.

The man smiled, but his eyes were cold and dead.

"I had one of our operators monitor it. To make sure there was no interference."

Shane still didn't speak.

"Then it was clear, Mr. Lockwood?"

"Very clear," Shane said in a low voice.

"Excellent."

They stood looking at each other.

Finally, Shane spoke.

"Then she heard every word I said."

The man bowed his head slightly.

"You'll pardon me. But I believe she did."

He turned abruptly and went to the door and paused there.

"Oh. Why stay in your suite on such a beautiful day?"

"And?"

"Why don't you go outdoors for a walk?"

"A walk?"

"Yes."

"Any suggestions?"

The man smiled at him again.

"Why don't you stroll to the piazza?"

"San Marco?"

"Exactly."

Shane waited for the man to speak again.

How much are you being paid? he thought.

How much?

This is Venice.

Beautiful, glorious Venice.

With its old classic bridges, its historic canals, its vaporettos.

Gondolas gliding through moonlit nights.

This is Italy.

Italy, glowing in the warm sunshine.

But beneath the soft glow there could be savage death.

Lying there.

Waiting silently.

Italy.

But is it much different in my country?

Is it?

Money corrupts there, money corrupts here.

People get killed for money.

It doesn't really matter where they are.

It doesn't.

He heard the man speak.

"Sit down at one of the tables and enjoy the sunshine."

"In the beautiful square."

"Exactly. Enjoy the view of the doge's palace. It goes back many centuries."

22

"I've looked at it already."

"Do it again, Mr. Lockwood."

"How long should I sit there?"

"Oh. A half hour. An hour at the most."

"I understand."

"Will you do that?"

"Yes," Shane said.

Their eyes met and the man flinched.

"I'm terribly sorry," he said in a low voice.

"I'm sure you are."

The man shook his head.

A sad look came into his eyes.

"You don't understand."

"Don't I?"

The man reached out and touched Shane's hand gently.

"Life doesn't leave one much choice. Sometimes one is trapped in a corner and has to do . . . to do . . ."

His voice trailed out into silence.

"One doesn't have to do anything," Shane said harshly.

The man shook his head.

"You're young. You don't understand."

"I understand perfectly."

"You don't."

"Tell your wife I'm glad she enjoyed the concert," Shane said bitterly.

The man flushed.

"I shall," he murmured.

Then he opened the door and went out.

Silence came flowing into the room.

Shane stood tall and motionless.

It's something more than the violin, he thought.

Something much more.

I can feel it.

What could it be?

Finally, he stirred and went out to the terrace and stood against the shining brass railing.

He looked down to the small pool.

It was empty.

The blond, long-haired girl was no longer in the shimmering water.

Then he saw her lying on a beach lounge, reading a book.

She was tall and shapely.

He leaned against the railing, looking down at her.

The sun was now out strong.

But he felt chilled.

Chapter

7

He sat at one of the outer tables drinking a Perrier.

It was his second.

He looked at his watch.

He had been sitting there close to an hour.

His throat dry.

His hands damp.

The historic square was crowded with summer tourists. The air was bright and clear and the throngs of pigeons, the famous St. Mark's pigeons, were glowing in the bright and hard sun.

The campanile rose pink into a soft blue sky.

Shane set the glass down on the hard surface of the table, and it was then that he heard the voice.

"Mind if I sit with you?"

He looked up.

A tall man, almost as tall as he was, lithe and tanned, with iron-gray, wavy hair, stood at his table.

He had a lean face, with sharp features and quiet brown eyes.

A clipped gray mustache.

Shane didn't answer.

The man wore a dark blue blazer with white slacks. The sun glittered off the gold buttons on his jacket.

Shane heard the voice again.

"I'm sure you don't mind."

It was the same voice of the night.

The man sat down and motioned crisply to a waiter. He ordered in Italian and then turned and smiled at Shane.

"Were you waiting long?"

"Not too long."

"I'm glad. Americans are an impatient lot. Don't you think?"

"I don't know."

"But of course we are. Have you ever been on a crowded New York street?"

"Yes."

"Waiting to grab a taxi? Or get onto a bus?"

Shane nodded.

"Then you know. We're all the same all over the country. Chicago, Los Angeles, San Francisco, Seattle. The same. Always the same desperate impatience to get there. And there is often nowhere. Isn't that so?"

And where do you want to go? Shane thought grimly. Where?

Taking me along with you.

The waiter brought a glass of white wine, set it down delicately on the table and went off.

The man held the glass up to the blazing sun.

"I love to see wine sparkle. I'm Arthur Kent."

He sipped the wine tentatively, nodded approvingly, and then drank.

"And you are, of course, Shane Lockwood."

"You know I am."

"Yes. I know."

He smiled and then spoke again.

"I've followed your career with great interest. Very great interest."

"I'm sure you have."

"I was in Amsterdam to hear you. And then I followed you here."

"Just to hear me perform."

"Just that."

"Am I that good?"

The man laughed.

It was a gentle, pleasant laugh.

"Oh, you play divinely."

Divinely.

And now you're playing with me.

Like a delicately cruel cat with a frightened mouse.

And you're enjoying it.

Kent sipped his wine and then put the glass down again, and Shane noticed for the first time the small diamond ring on one of the supple fingers.

The ring glittered in the sun.

With a hard glitter.

And then Shane saw that the tip of the finger was gone.

He heard the man's low, soft voice.

"Would you believe that when I was your age I was preparing for a bright career in concert music?"

"No."

"But you must."

"What instrument?"

"Violin, of course."

"Of course."

Shane waited for the man to speak again.

"I was exactly your age."

"And?"

"And something happened to one of my fingers. The left hand. You know how vital the left hand is to a violinist."

We both know, don't we?

"A terrible accident. Terrible and yet trivial. I was cutting, of all things, a cucumber. Making a salad. And the knife slipped and sliced off the top of this finger."

He held it up.

The ring glittered.

The rim of the finger was white and dead.

A cold, cruel look had come into the brown eyes.

"I couldn't play anymore."

He paused and then went on.

"My career went up in flames. Would you believe that?"

No, Shane thought.

You're lying.

You're out to terrify me.

You are.

You never were a violinist.

Never. And that is not how you lost the tip of your finger.

The man leaned a bit toward Shane.

A knowing look on his lean face.

As if he could read Shane's thoughts.

"Whether you believe me or not does not really matter. Does it?"

Shane didn't answer.

28

"We artists are constantly walking along the edge. Isn't that so?"

Shane was silent.

"And sometimes we fall off. Or are pushed off. Down, down from the heights. To be smashed below."

Shane pressed his lips tightly together.

"Smashed," Kent said again. "And we are through. For good. Finished. Never to come back to the heights again. Never."

Shane's hand closed into a hard fist.

What is it you want?

What?

Tell me.

He heard the voice again.

"The applause ends. The adulation. Finished. *La commedia è finita.*"

The man stopped speaking and looked away from Shane, his quiet brown eyes surveying the square.

The pigeons suddenly rose, as if on command, and flew in whirring circles around the square.

Shane watched them dully.

"I'm going to ask you to do me a great favor," Kent said.

"What is it?"

The man slowly turned back to Shane.

"I'm sure you won't refuse me."

"What do you want me to do?"

The man's thin lips pressed together and he looked long at Shane.

"Well?" Shane asked.

The man slowly shook his head.

"I'll let you know when it's time for you to know."

29

"I want to know now," Shane said in a harsh voice. "Now."

The cold, cruel look came back into Kent's eyes.

"Would you like to see your precious violin again? The Guarnerius?"

"You know I would."

"In one piece? Or shattered into fragments?"

Shane paled.

"Well, Lockwood?"

"You wouldn't do that. You couldn't."

The man nodded slowly.

"Oh, but I could."

"Only a savage would do a thing like that."

The man laughed softly.

But this time it was not a pleasant laugh.

"I've never considered myself anything but a savage. Does that surprise you, Lockwood?"

"That violin goes back centuries. It's a supreme work of art. It's . . ."

And he couldn't go on.

"Irreplaceable?"

"Yes. Yes."

"I know that very well. That's why I took it from you."

Shane tensed and leaned forward toward the man.

"How much money do you want? How much?"

Kent smiled and shook his head.

"Not a cent."

"What?"

"Just the favor."

"Only that?" Shane murmured.

"Correct."

30

Kent finished his wine and then set the glass down on the table.

A slow, deliberate gesture.

Shane waited in silence.

Finally, the man spoke again.

"When are you booked to fly home?"

"Tomorrow. I'm sure you know that already."

"Tomorrow is Friday. Change the flight to Sunday noon."

"Why?"

But the man didn't answer him.

He took a cigarette out of a silver case, lit it, and then sat there smoking and gazing about him.

When he spoke again, it was in a soft, meditative voice.

"Do you know how many celebrated figures sat in this historic square?"

Shane didn't answer him.

Kent inhaled and then let the smoke out through his fine nostrils, in two thin blue streams.

"Lord Byron, the great English poet, may have sat in the very same chair you are sitting in now. At his side, the beautiful Countess Guiccioli. Did you know that, Lockwood?"

He didn't wait for an answer.

"In this century, Thomas Mann, the master novelist. Did you ever read his novella, *Death in Venice*?"

Again he didn't wait for an answer.

"Mahler, the noted composer. Do you like his work? Oh, so many celebrated figures sat here. So many."

He smiled.

"And now Arthur Kent, the failed violinist, sits with

you and asks you for a favor. History moves on, doesn't it?"

He snuffed out his cigarette and slowly got up.

His shadow fell long and sharp onto the pavement.

"Lockwood."

"Yes."

The man pointed to the campanile, rising into the pure sapphire sky.

The sun high above it.

"Did you know that in the fifteenth century, men were hung in wooden cages from that magnificent tower? Sometimes as long as a full year on hard bread and stinking water? Some died of slow starvation, some went mad, some screamed all the time, some prayed fervently all through the interminable hours. While below them people, oh so fashionably dressed, walked up and down the huge square, up and down, smiling and indifferent. Scarcely looking up at the tortured souls in the cages above them."

He paused and went on.

"Do you think the fifteenth century was any crueler than our century? Do you?"

Shane didn't answer.

Kent's voice became hard and metallic.

"Don't make any foolish moves. Or you'll regret them terribly."

His eyes pierced Shane.

"You'll be watched all the time. The stakes are too high. You've no idea how high. Don't force me to become savage and cruel to you. You play too divinely for that. I want to enjoy your fall concert at Lincoln Center. Is that clear?"

Shane nodded.

"Yes," Shane murmured.

"You'll hear from me again."

Then the man walked away from Shane.

Chapter

8

He was walking along, a desolate feeling within him, when he saw her.

He stood there and didn't move.

His gray eyes upon her.

Later on, he would say to himself with bitterness, We are creatures of chance. We have no control over our lives, our destinies.

None whatsoever.

It happens and there is nothing we can do about it.

Nothing.

You meet a girl and your life is changed.

And it doesn't matter how young or old you are.

You meet a girl . . .

He would say that with bitterness.

And heartbreak.

Later on.

But now as he looked up at her, a sudden glow began within him.

Warm and spreading.

Driving out the desolation.

And he didn't know why.

She was standing near one of the weathered balustrades of the old Rialto Bridge, an open sketchbook in her hand.

He stood there watching her.

She gazed out over the sparkling waters of the canal and then bent her head, the long blond hair stirring in the soft breeze, and continued sketching on the gleaming white paper.

A stream of tourists passed by her and soon the bridge was fairly deserted.

He went up and stood silently, a few yards from her, but near enough to see the pencil lines in the sketch.

The sun glinted off the ends of the blond hair.

Now that he was close to her, he could see her fine profile.

She is very attractive, he thought.

About my age.

Give or take a year.

She could be a college student on a summer art trip.

Lots of them are here from all over Europe.

What better place to come for that than Venice?

An American college student.

How do I know that she's American?

Well, because . . .

I really don't know.

Suddenly he heard her voice.

It was soft and friendly.

"I'm trying to get that old white palace over there."

"I know."

"The lines shimmer in the sun."

"Uh-huh."

35

She is American.

"Tough to do."

"It is," he nodded.

She paused and looked over at him for the first time.

Her eyes were large and brown, almost golden in the sun.

"Am I getting them?"

He came a bit closer and stood by her, studying the sketch.

"I think so," he said.

She smiled gratefully at him and continued sketching.

"It's the Palace San Stefano. Did you know that?"

"No."

"Lots of history in it. This whole city is full of history."

"It is."

"History and mystery. That's a poor rhyme. Aren't you Shane Lockwood?"

He felt his face redden just a bit.

"I guess I am."

"I'm Laurie Carson. We're at the same hotel."

"I know. I was watching you swim this morning."

"Were you?"

She stopped sketching and looked up at him.

She was tall, but she was still a few inches shorter than he was.

"So you were watching me?"

"Yes."

A playful smile came into the gentle brown eyes.

"Which do I do better? Sketch or swim?"

"Both."

"Really?"

"That's right."

She laughed softly.

"And which do I look better in? My bathing suit or these old jeans and sloppy shirt?"

"Both."

She shook her head, her long hair swinging in the sun.

"Blarney. That's your Irish blarney."

He grinned.

"Are you Irish?"

"Why do you ask?"

"I just get the feeling that you are."

She nodded.

"In a way. One of my grandmothers came from county Kerry."

"Is that a fact?"

"It is."

"Or are you putting me on?"

"Why should I be putting you on?"

He shrugged.

"I don't know."

She smiled and turned back to her sketching.

He watched her for a while and then spoke again.

He felt good being by her.

It made him forget.

"My Dad's father came from county Kerry," he said. "My mother's came out of Cork."

"All the saints come from Kerry."

"Who told you that?"

"Grandma."

He laughed.

"Grandfather was no saint. Not by a long shot. I was named after him."

"His name was Shane?"

He shook his head.

"Sean. My mother changed it to Shane."

"Which do you like?"

"I'll stay with Shane."

"Because you're stuck with it?"

"No. Just like it better."

"Honest?"

"Honest."

"I like Sean better."

"Why?"

"I don't know. Just like it better."

Yes, he thought. One likes things and doesn't know why.

One falls in love and doesn't know why.

It just happens that way.

Dad told me how it happened to him and Mom. He just saw her and was hooked.

And he didn't know why.

But it took a while before she began to really love him.

I guess that's how it is.

A white vaporetto passed by silently, the passengers sitting motionless, almost like statues.

They both stood there watching the boat glide along till it disappeared into the golden haze of the day.

Shane stood close to Laurie, feeling her fragrance.

A gentle, pervasive fragrance.

She stirred and spoke.

"And you're no saint?"

"I sure am not."

"You say that with a great joy."

"Do I?"

38

"Uh-huh."

"Well," he said. "I find the lives of saints pretty dull."

"And your grandfather felt the same way."

He nodded.

"He kicked over the traces every now and then."

"And had a good time doing it."

"He did."

"And you?"

"I kick them over at times."

She looked at him.

"I'll bet you do," she said softly.

And then they both laughed.

It was at that instant that he saw the man leaning against the far end of the bridge.

Leaning casually against one of the balustrades.

Arms folded.

His smooth black hair gleaming in the sun.

He wore a white suit.

And he was watching them.

Shane was sure of that.

A mixed feeling of anger and fear swept through him.

He tensed up.

The girl glanced up from the sketch pad and noticed the change in him.

"Shane?"

"Yes?"

"Anything the matter?"

He was still looking at the man.

"What?"

"You seemed to . . ."

She stopped speaking.

He slowly turned back to her.

39

"No, Laurie. It's nothing."

"Are you sure?"

"Yes."

Then he began smiling again.

She gazed up at him, her eyes trying to probe within.

He thought she was about to speak.

But she silently turned back to her sketching again.

He stood there watching her work, yet all the time aware of the man in the white suit.

She is talented, he thought.

She has the feel of a good artist.

Very good.

Suddenly she spoke again, while still sketching.

"Would you like to have dinner with me tonight?"

"With you?"

"I know a nice little restaurant. Not too far from the hotel. We can walk over there in ten minutes."

"Oh."

"Well?"

"Sure," he said.

"We'll split the bill. Okay with you?"

"I'd rather take care of it."

"Split."

"You win."

"Seven o'clock?"

And he sensed that she wanted him to leave her.

"Good enough, Laurie."

She smiled at him.

"I'll be waiting in the hotel lobby."

"I'll be there," he said.

"Just dress casual. It's a friendly place. Simple food."

"Simple food, but good."

40

She nodded.

"That's it."

"Okay with me."

She held out her hand to him and he took it.

"So long, Shane."

He let her warm hand go almost reluctantly.

"So long, Laurie," he said.

Then he turned and walked slowly toward the man in the white suit and as he neared him, he could see his face more clearly.

A harsh, tight face.

With small dark eyes.

The man stood there quietly, almost insolently, looking at him.

Shane was about to walk past him, when suddenly he stopped and stared harshly at the man.

Their eyes met.

For an instant, blazing anger swept through Shane.

"What do you want?"

The man didn't answer.

"Tell me."

The man still didn't answer.

"You understand me. I can see you do."

And Shane felt a sudden, mad urge to grab the man, lift him, and throw him into the canal below.

He stood there, his muscles tight and hard, and fought for control.

Looming over the man.

Then he suddenly breathed out, straightened up, and walked quickly away.

His hands still clenched.

Somehow he felt that Laurie had stopped sketching

and had been standing there tensely, fearfully watching him.

But he didn't turn around.

Just kept walking.

The sun beating down on him relentlessly.

Chapter

9

He went out to Lido Beach to sit on a chair on the sands and gaze out at the blue waters of the Adriatic Sea.

He had always loved beaches and water.

He was a strong swimmer; back home he had gone out many times a mile or so into the broad Pacific, just to get the feeling of being alone, completely and securely alone.

He would lie on his back, look up at the glowing sky, and go over difficult passages in some of the concertos.

And now as he sat there near the Adriatic, the horizon stretching out calm and eternal before him, a sense of peace and perspective came over him.

He was able to see things as they were.

With a chilling clarity.

I'm in trouble, he said to himself.

Deep trouble.

It was not of my making.

It happened.

Just happened.

And there is nothing to do but go along with it for the while.

It's much too dangerous to try to do anything.

I just have to wait for them.

Wait.

Kent has all the moves now.

All of them.

Wait.

Shane leaned back in the chair and stared out at the sparkling sea.

He watched a tall blond girl standing alone on a corner of the beach, the sun gilding her hair, and he instantly thought of Laurie.

Laurie Carson.

Is Carson an Irish name?

Of course it is.

Has to be.

But then again, she's only part Irish.

So what?

Some people tell me that Lockwood isn't an Irish name.

One of the critics wrote that I couldn't be Irish because the Irish have never had truly outstanding concert violinists.

Only a critic would say that.

Another fellow wrote that I was built more like a football player than a violinist.

How is a violinist supposed to be built?

I wanted to write him a letter but never got around to it.

Shane kept looking at the blond girl.

Laurie Carson.

I've just met her and I can't stop thinking about her.

Just can't.

She comes weaving into my thoughts.

That's how my father said it happened to him.

Must be in the genes.

I've never felt this way before.

I've gone out with lots of girls but . . .

Never felt this way before.

Shane looked away from the girl and out along the glittering stretch of water.

Can't wait till I see her tonight.

And yet.

I must be careful.

Careful that I don't drag her into my trouble.

Yes, I must not . . .

"Mr. Lockwood?"

He looked away from the blue sea and up in front of him.

A woman was standing there, outlined against the sun.

"Do you remember me?"

He didn't answer.

"Do you mind if I sit next to you for a few minutes?"

"No," he said.

It was the well-dressed, gray-haired woman who had stopped him as he walked along the Grand Canal.

The night of the concert.

She had asked him for an autograph.

While far behind her, in the darkness, stood the figure of the motionless man.

Silently watching them.

And now he knew that the man was Arthur Kent.

"Elaine Stark," he said.

"Without the E."

"Without the E," he softly echoed.

"You do remember."

"Yes."

It was Arthur Kent.

I'm sure of that now.

Shane quietly studied the woman.

She was now wearing a fashionable white dress and white shoes.

She smiled, took off her dark sunglasses, and sat down on a chair next to him.

"I was walking the beach and suddenly I saw you. Sitting alone. Do you often sit alone?"

"Yes."

"I guess all artists like their privacy."

"Gives us time to think."

"I'm sure it does."

She took off her straw hat and put it on her lap.

The two sat silently.

He waited.

And as he did, he glanced at her.

She still has fine features, he thought.

She must have been a very attractive woman when she was younger.

For some strange reason she makes me think of Laurie.

The same delicately shaped profile.

Oval face.

Yet her eyes are very dark, almost brooding, while Laurie's eyes are almost golden.

Golden and smiling.

A breeze came softly over them, the woman smoothed

her hair down, and then the air was quiet and calm again.

I would say she's in her mid-fifties.

That would be about Arthur Kent's age.

Shane looked down at the diamond bracelet the woman wore on her slender left wrist.

It sparkled in the sun.

With a cold sparkle.

You've come with a purpose, he thought.

What is it?

He sat there waiting for her to speak.

Out on the water, far out, almost to the horizon, he could barely make out the white of a sail.

It seemed motionless.

Pale white against a glittering blue.

He watched it for a while.

Suddenly he wished to be out there on the boat, away from everything.

Just lying on the deck with the sun streaming down upon him.

Time coming to a dead stop.

Suddenly he heard the woman speak.

In a soft, low voice.

All the time she faced the eternal sea.

Never once did she turn to Shane.

"He is capable of murder," she said.

Shane felt a chill go through him.

"I know. I have seen him do it."

And then she was silent again.

Her face was now white and drawn.

She put her hand on his and let it rest there.

The hand was cold to the touch.

She began to speak again.

"I was against drawing you into this from the very beginning. But he would not listen to me."

She paused and then went on.

"That was the first time he ever went against my wishes. The first time. He would not listen."

She pressed his hand gently.

"You're in. And there is nothing I can do about it. But I will do my best to protect you. I still have some influence on Arthur Kent."

"What does he want me to do?"

She shook her head.

"I can't tell you. He's setting everything up. You'll know soon enough."

"What if I don't want to go along with it?"

"You'll die," she said softly.

He looked away from her and out to the white sail.

There was another silence.

He finally broke it.

"The Guarnerius?"

"You'll get it back when it's all over. Untouched. I promise you that."

"Can I believe you?" he asked bitterly.

"You can," she said.

Out on the sea the sail began to move slowly and then glide over the water.

He sat there watching it.

Then she spoke again.

"Just do as he says. Always remember that."

Shane didn't speak.

"In a way I'm putting my life on the line for you, Shane. So trust me."

She had turned to him and he thought he could see the hint of tears in the dark, brooding eyes.

48

But he wasn't sure.

"Why are you doing it?" he asked.

"We are being watched now. But Arthur will not be told I came here to talk to you. The man watching us is on my side in this."

He looked from her to the figures walking the beach. Then he turned back to her.

"You haven't answered my question."

"Call me Elaine."

"Elaine. You still haven't answered."

She gently pressed his hand.

"And I won't."

"But you must . . ."

And his voice trailed away into silence.

"Just leave it as it is," she said.

"I wish you would tell me."

She shook her head and rose.

"Please."

She stood a while gazing out to the sea, and then she finally turned to him.

"That attractive girl you were talking to on the Rialto Bridge."

He trembled slightly.

"Yes?"

"You seemed to like her."

He didn't speak.

"And she seems taken with you. Isn't that so?"

A sad smile came onto the woman's lips.

"You're seeing her tonight for dinner," she said.

He stared at her.

"How did you know that?"

"The man in the white suit."

"What about him?"

The smile was no longer on her lips.

She hesitated a while and then spoke.

"Let's say he either reads lips expertly or he has exceptional hearing."

Later on, Shane would vividly remember those words.

Later on.

When it was all too late.

Much too late.

Now he heard Elaine Stark's voice again.

"You can continue to see her. But . . ."

"But what?"

The woman looked down to her diamond bracelet and then spoke.

"Always remember what I said to you."

"I'll keep her out of this."

"You'll make sure of that?"

"Yes."

"Not a word or hint to her or anybody else."

"It will be that way."

"You give me your promise?"

He nodded.

They were silent.

The diamonds glittered in the sun.

"I believe you, Shane," she said.

And then she turned and left him.

He watched her till she disappeared into the golden haze of the afternoon. But for some reason the glittering diamonds stayed on in his eyes and mind.

Glittering.

Ever glittering.

Chapter

10

He was lying on the bed, fully clothed, looking up at the ceiling when the phone rang.

He reached over with his long hand and picked up the receiver.

The rays of the evening sun filtered into the room and onto the black receiver.

Staining it red.

He looked over to the clock on the night table.

It showed ten minutes to seven.

He was meeting Laurie at seven.

"Mr. Lockwood?"

It was the smooth voice of the hotel operator.

"Yes?"

"I have a call for you from Santa Barbara, California."

"I'll take it," he said.

"All right."

I'll take it and you'll be listening, he thought sardonically.

51

Then he heard his father's voice.

"Shane?"

"Yes, Dad."

"How're things?"

He hesitated an instant and then answered.

"Going along."

"How were the reviews?"

"Quite good. The *Herald Tribune* gave me a blast."

"A blast?"

"I mean they praised it quite a bit."

"Oh. That's fine. Very fine."

There was a slight pause and then his father spoke again.

"I have time now to talk. I felt that you wanted to say something to me during our last call."

"And it's been on your mind, Dad."

"It has, Shane. I kind of hurried off the phone."

"You had surgery waiting."

"Just the same I could've . . . I should've called you back after I was done. But I didn't."

"Well, now we're speaking again."

"There was something troubling you."

"Troubling me?"

"Yes, Shane."

Shane looked out the window at the pink-streaked sky and was silent.

And then he heard his father's voice again.

"There was something wrong. I kind of felt it. Underneath everything."

"Oh," Shane said gently.

"You know, a father senses these things. If he cares for his son."

And you care for me, Shane thought.

But I'm going it alone, Dad.

Alone.

It's the only way to go now.

"Well, Shane?"

Shane lay back and didn't speak.

"Shane?"

"I'm here."

"Well?"

"It has to do with a girl," Shane said.

"A girl?"

"Uh-huh."

"Are you serious?"

"Serious? How do you mean?"

"I . . . I guess I don't know what I mean."

He could see his father's perplexed face and it made him smile.

"I met her," he said. "And something strange is happening to me."

"Strange?"

"Yes. Just spoke to her a little while and I can't get her out of my mind."

There was a silence.

"Dad, are you there?"

"Yes, Shane."

"When you met Mom the first time. The bells started ringing. Isn't that so? That's what you once said to me."

"Yes. That's so."

"But you were somewhat older than I am now."

"I was."

"How much?"

"Oh, a few years, Shane. Now, Son, I . . . I . . ."

And his voice faded away.

"I just can't get her out of my mind. Kind of weird, isn't it?"

"Yes," he heard his father murmur.

"But that's how it happens. Right?"

"I don't know, Shane. I just don't know."

And he could tell that his father was completely bewildered.

"Dad?"

"I'm here, Shane."

"How's Mom?"

"Fine. Just fine. Busy with her affairs."

"That sounds like Mom."

And Shane laughed.

"She'll probably run for Congress one of these days," his father said.

"I'll bet she will. And get in."

And Shane laughed again.

He was feeling light-headed.

"Shane, let's talk a little while."

"I'd love to. But I've got to sign off. It's five to seven."

"What does that mean?"

"I've got a date at seven."

"With the girl?"

"That's it."

"But . . ."

Shane cut in.

"Thanks for calling. You've helped me a lot."

"Have I?"

"Yes."

"How?"

"Oh, just talking to you. Hearing your voice."

There was a silence.

54

"Give Mom my regards."

"I will."

"Good-bye, Dad."

"But, Shane, I . . ."

"Got to go. How's the weather out there?"

"The weather? It's raining."

"Sunny out here. Good-bye, Dad."

"Good-bye, Shane."

He heard the click.

And then he laughed.

He put the black receiver back down onto its cradle and then lay there idly gazing at it.

The dying rays of the sun flecked the black.

Deep, deep in the recesses of his mind, a thought came weaving in, a thought of dark, spilled blood.

Chapter

11

He was standing in the crowded, noisy lobby when he saw her weave her way through and come walking over to him, and with each step she took he felt his heart quiver.

This is no good, he said.

Just no good.

And then.

Why not?

Why shouldn't it be good?

"Shane?"

"Laurie?"

They stood there silently looking at each other, unaware of the people passing by them.

She wore a flowered-print blouse open at the collar and a short black skirt. Her shoes were a shiny black.

Her blond hair was drawn back tightly and braided at the back of her neck.

Does it make her look younger or older? he wondered.

I don't know.

She is about my age.

I'm sure of that.

And what makes me so sure?

What?

She is my age and let it go at that.

And if she isn't, what does it matter?

"You said dress casually," he said.

"I did. And you listened. I like your outfit."

He had on a Ralph Lauren polo shirt, light blue, and light blue slacks and light tan loafers.

He stood there, broad and handsome, looking down at her.

"I like yours, too," he said. "Like it a lot."

She smiled, pleased.

"It's really nothing. Just something hanging around in the closet."

"Uh-huh."

And he thought, You could wear an old flour sack and still look beautiful to me.

You sure could.

He heard her speak.

"Hungry?"

"Very."

She laughed.

"Okay. I'm hungry, too. Let's go."

"You lead the way, Laurie."

She nodded and they went out of the bustling lobby and onto the quiet cobblestones, and as they walked along the canal, talking casually, he suddenly remembered the night of the concert, when a woman came out of the darkness and swung his life around.

Without his knowing it.

57

His face tightened.

A dark look came into the gray eyes.

He didn't speak for a while.

She glanced up at him.

"Are you a moody person?"

"What?"

"Most artists are."

"No. I'm not," he said. "Not at all."

They walked along.

He spoke again.

"And I'm not an artist. I'm a fiddle player. Nothing more or less than that."

"Just that?"

"Right."

"Would you say a good fiddle player?"

"All right. I'd say that."

An impish smile came into the brown eyes.

"How about a very fine fiddle player?"

"Let's stop at good. That's how I see it."

"But some critics don't see it that way."

"What do you mean?"

"Some of them seem to think you're a great fiddle player."

He grinned. "Don't listen to the critics."

"I don't. I've heard you play."

"Where?"

"I've heard you. Let's walk."

They had stopped and now he linked his arm in hers, and they walked along and he felt happy just being with her.

"You're not moody," she said. "But you're thoughtful. You sit by yourself and think things out for hours on end."

58

"Not for hours on end. But I do that. How about you?"

She laughed softly.

"But I'm not an artist."

"Oh, I think you are. Your work is quite good. What I've seen of it."

"You've seen very little."

"But enough to know."

"I still have a long, long way to go, Shane. You're there already."

He shook his head.

"I'm not, Laurie. But tell me, are you moody?"

"Is it important to you?"

They had stopped walking.

"Yes," he said.

"Why?"

"Just is."

He felt her fragrance about him.

"Then the answer is yes."

"I don't believe you."

She looked at him and laughed.

"All artists are moody. It comes with the territory. And you just made me an artist."

"Did I?"

And he laughed, too.

He stood close to her.

There was still a glow, a slowly dying glow, in the western sky and the waters of the canal began to glimmer with soft bronze tints.

The old palaces lining the canal took on an almost mystical aura.

Their reflections shimmered in the water.

He thought of the Palace of San Stefano and her standing before it, sketching.

The two watched the fading sunset.

And as they stood there a gentle darkness came softly down upon them.

Laurie, he whispered to himself.

He thought of the Rialto Bridge and Shakespeare.

And then his mind fled to Verona.

To the star-crossed lovers.

Young.

So very young.

And we are young, Laurie.

He suddenly wanted to draw her into his arms and kiss her.

He felt that this is what she would want.

But then he heard her speak.

"Have you ever been out to Lido?"

A strange chill came over him.

He almost shivered.

Shane stared at Laurie.

The shadows of the oncoming night had crept over her oval face.

The golden eyes had become dark.

So very dark.

For an instant he thought he was looking at a mask.

Then he drove the thought away.

And he saw her as she was.

"Why do you ask?"

"Oh, everybody goes out there one time or another."

He didn't speak.

"I like to go out there and walk on the beach."

"Yes," he murmured.

"And I do some sketching there."

"I guess you do."

She was standing looking at him.

A puzzled expression on her face.

"Is there anything wrong, Shane?"

"What?"

"A change seems to have come over you."

He shook his head.

"No. Nothing at all."

"You sure?"

"Yes."

Her eyes were still searching him out.

He began to smile.

"Let's get going," he said.

Slowly, hesitantly, she nodded.

"All right," she said gently.

Laurie linked her arm in his and they began to walk.

But he was back again at Lido Beach and hearing Elaine Stark's words to him.

If you don't do as he says, you'll die.

Chapter

12

The restaurant overlooked one of the narrow, winding waterways that led from the Grand Canal.

"I live in the Village," she said.

"Greenwich Village?"

"Yes. I go to NYU. Washington Square."

He nodded.

They were sitting in the tiny outdoor garden of the restaurant, between small trees with trembling leaves. Above them, there was a deep blue sky with a faint sprinkling of stars.

A soft breeze came over the canal and to them.

Soft and warm.

In the distance they heard the voice of a singing gondolier.

A thin, tenor voice.

You're wretchedly off-key, Shane thought.

And yet I like hearing you.

Just as I like listening to Laurie's low, intimate voice.

Somehow I feel that I will never forget this night.

"I just roll out of bed in the morning, walk a few blocks, and I'm in class. Nothing can beat that, Shane."

He laughed.

"Nothing can."

Then they became silent, drinking their coffee, and he listened to the fading voice of the gondolier and he thought again of Verona.

Of Romeo Montague and Juliet Capulet.

They were young, he thought, so very young.

Romeo just looked at her and instantly fell in love.

And she with him.

Romeo.

Juliet.

Verona.

Venice.

Italy.

All things happen in sunny, romantic Italy.

Life, love and . . .

Death.

He put down the glistening cup and looked across the small table at her.

The candlelight flickered in the soft breeze.

It gave her face a gentle glow.

You're beautiful, Julie, he said to himself.

Deep in my heart I shall always call you Julie.

Always that.

He heard himself speak.

"Your folks come from New York?"

She shook her head and the candlelight glinted off her blond hair.

"No. Dad comes from Chicago. And my mother from Baltimore."

"And where did you grow up?"

"Baltimore. My mother still lives there."

"And your father?"

"He went back to Chicago. He's the CEO of a big corporation."

"They split?"

"Just a few years ago. They both live alone in big houses. No new marriages. Doesn't make sense. Just doesn't."

And he wanted to say to her, A lot of things don't make sense.

They just don't.

They happen and you don't know why they happen. You don't.

He heard her voice.

"How about your parents, Shane?"

"Mine? They're still together."

She looked across the table at him.

"They still love each other?"

"I believe they do," he said.

"That's nice," she said.

"It is."

"But are you sure?"

"Yes, Laurie."

A wistful look had come into her eyes.

"It's a shame when love dies," she said in a low voice.

He was silent.

"I think it's worse than real death. Don't you, Shane?"

"Yes," he said gently.

Her finger played with the glistening rim of the cup. Then she spoke.

"When I was out visiting him, I asked him what happened."

She sighed softly.

"What did he say?"

She shrugged.

"He didn't speak for a while. And then he said, 'I don't know, Laurie. I honestly don't know. Just woke up one morning and I said to myself, I don't love her anymore. I don't.' "

"And your mother?"

"She just put her lips together and didn't speak."

"Never told you?"

"Never."

He thought she was going to cry so he put his hand onto hers.

She let it rest there.

She spoke again, in a very low voice.

"People shouldn't fall in love with each other if they intend to break up. They shouldn't."

And then she looked up at him and sadly smiled.

"That doesn't make sense when you think it out."

"It does, Laurie," he said.

"No. It's nonsense. Let's go. All right, Shane?"

"Sure."

They quibbled over the bill and finally he had to let it be her way and they split it.

Then they left the restaurant.

Chapter

13

They walked silently along the narrow, winding canal, and he had the very strange sensation that he was back centuries ago, walking the night with Juliet, alone, so absolutely alone, just he and Juliet.

He glanced at her. Her hair shone softly.

Julie.

Julie.

They came to a small footbridge.

They stopped.

"When are you going home, Shane?" she asked.

"Sunday."

They were alone in the sheltering shadow of the small arch.

The old buildings lining the canal loomed above them, dark and silent.

The only sound was the quiet lapping of the water.

Quiet and eternal.

"So soon?"

And disappointment was in her voice.

"Yes."

"You have to go?"

And he wanted to say, No, I can stay as long as you want.

As long as that.

But the lean, grim figure of Arthur Kent stood before him.

"I'm afraid I'll have to."

"Oh," she said, and no more.

"How about you, Laurie?"

"I'll be here another week."

"I see."

"I've been in Venice over a month. I'll be going back to New York."

"To your apartment in the Village?"

"Yes."

"You like the Village?"

"Very much."

"Why?"

"Well, Shane, the people. The atmosphere."

"I know what you mean," he said.

"You've been there?"

He nodded.

"Many times."

She smiled.

"I like to sit in Washington Square Park on a sunny day. It's so alive. Just bubbling."

He grinned.

"I know what you mean."

She looked up at him.

"Maybe we'll sit there together some time?"

"Yes, Laurie," he said. "We will."

They were silent.

Listening to the soft sound of the water.

The soft magical sound.

We're alone, he thought.

So very alone.

As if no one else existed in the world.

Just we two and this magical night.

He drew close to her.

She had begun to speak, but he didn't hear her.

"We could go to some galleries on Houston Street and . . ."

She stopped speaking.

He drew her to him.

"Laurie," he whispered.

"Shane."

Her voice trembled.

Her arms were about him and they kissed.

Then he felt the night enclosing them and all he could hear was the soft, incessant sound of the water and far, far in the distance, the sad tolling of a church bell.

Chapter

14

He was sitting on the terrace, gazing out at the still, starry sky, still feeling her lips on his, when he heard the soft turning of the lock in the door of the suite and then the door quietly opening and closing.

He rose from his seat and stood there, tense and waiting.

The apartment was in complete darkness.

Then he saw the shadowy figure come slowly across the large room and stop at the threshold of the terrace.

He saw the glittering eyes.

Glittering in the starlight.

It was Arthur Kent.

He carried a black violin case in his right hand.

The Guarnerius case.

"I see you are finally back in your suite. Did you have a good time?"

Shane didn't answer.

He pressed his lips together grimly.

"I was waiting for you in the hotel bar."

"What do you want?" he asked.

"Just to have a talk."

Kent set the violin case on the terrazzo floor and then went over to a lamp and flicked it on.

His lean, tight face came into being.

"Come in and sit down, Lockwood."

Shane silently went into the room and over to a chair.

He kept looking at the violin case.

And as he looked he realized how desperately he missed holding the Guarnerius in his hands.

Holding it and playing it.

Hearing once again its rich and unique melody.

An ache settled into Shane's being.

His hands trembled.

Kent watched him and smiled sardonically.

"It's there in your poignant eyes. That violin is part of your life, isn't it? An extremely vital part."

Shane felt his heart begin to pound.

And then he heard the man speak again.

"Possibly it's all of your life. No matter whom you fall in love with, that Guarnerius will always be first in your heart. Before anything or anybody else. Isn't that so, Lockwood? How could it be otherwise?"

Shane clenched his hands into fists and didn't speak.

Within him an uncontrollable rage was building.

He heard the man's quiet voice.

"You could break me apart at this moment, couldn't you?"

"Why did you bring it here?"

"To return it?"

Shane shook his head.

"You wouldn't. Not until you got what you wanted."

"That's correct, Lockwood. I wouldn't."

Kent smiled and that cruel smile set Shane off.

He sprang up from his chair and started walking to the man.

His face tight with rage.

"I'm taking that violin from you. Do you hear me?"

His voice rose and filled the room.

"Do you?"

Kent laughed softly.

Shane's rage overwhelmed him.

He reached down to grab the throat of the man, grab it and hold it tight in his big, fierce hands, when he saw the gun.

It gleamed in the semidarkness.

He stopped stock-still.

His breath coming short.

Then he took a step backward.

He heard the man's voice.

"It has a silencer on it, Lockwood."

Shane stared at the gun in the man's delicate but supple hand and he felt his heart begin to sink.

Sink into black despair.

He heard Kent's low voice.

Low and calm.

So very calm.

"One touch of the trigger and you'll die. A bullet shattering your skull. That fine, attractive face of yours covered with dripping blood. The career of Shane Lockwood, the brilliant young violinist, will come to a sudden and final end. No more concerts, my friend."

He paused.

A cold glint in his brown eyes.

"You'll lie here on that terrazzo floor stone-dead. And I'll walk out of here and lock the door again. And no one will ever know I visited you. No one. Do you still want to choke the life out of me?''

He laughed softly.

You enjoy torturing me, Shane thought bitterly.

You're nothing but a cultivated savage.

But you've told me that already.

You know what you are.

How well you know.

Shane turned away from the man and gazed at the impassive night sky.

There were tears of rage in his eyes.

Rage and despair.

He heard the man speak again.

Now the voice was icy and commanding.

''Lockwood.''

The man said his name again.

Shane slowly turned back to Kent.

''Don't ever let that Irish temper of yours take hold again. Remember what I say to you.''

He pointed to the chair.

The gun still gripped in his hand.

''Sit down again.''

Shane still didn't move.

How much I've come to hate you, he thought.

How very much.

''Do as I say, Lockwood.''

There was a fiery spurt from the gun and a small vase lay shattered on the floor.

''Well?''

Shane stared at the scattered fragments of the vase and then slowly sat down again.

''That's better.''

The silence of the night came into the room.

Finally, he heard the man speak again.

"I want you to do something for me. Tomorrow."

Shane waited.

"Tomorrow is really today, isn't it? It's close to morning now. How times goes. A French poet, Ronsard, once wrote, 'Time goes, you say? Ah, no, we go, Time stays.' Do you agree with that, Lockwood?"

Shane didn't answer.

Kent laughed softly.

Then spoke.

"You've certainly heard of Carlo Goldoni?"

"Yes," Shane murmured.

"I thought you would. He's one of Italy's best-loved playwrights. Comes from another century. A better one than ours, I assure you. Well, there is a statue. The Goldoni Statue. You surely know where it is. Everybody in Venice knows."

He paused and then went on.

"Italy honors its artists with statues. Our country forgets they ever lived."

Kent's fine lips thinned with contempt and then he spoke again.

"Not far from the statue is a small but noted museum. I want you to go there tomorrow."

You said tomorrow is today, Shane thought bleakly.

You make time meaningless.

Just as you're sure to make my life meaningless.

"Take your girlfriend with you."

"What?"

Shane had tautened.

Kent smiled.

"Why not, Lockwood? The museum has a fine collection of rare diamonds and other precious stones. I'm

73

sure she'll enjoy herself just looking at them. The most valuable piece is the Guiccioli Tiara.''

He paused.

A glow had come into the eyes.

As if he were looking at the tiara at that very moment.

"I want you both to see it," he said in a low, almost awed voice. "It's one of the world's masterpieces."

"Why do you want me to see it?"

"I'll tell you in due course."

"In due course," Shane echoed bitterly.

You keep holding me off.

You play with me with such cruelty.

Like a savage cat with its prey.

He heard the man's low voice.

"Lord Byron gave that treasure to his lover, Countess Teresa Guiccioli."

His voice lowered to a whisper.

"The tiara."

He stared at Shane but didn't seem to see him.

The glow was gone and a film had come over the large brown eyes.

Shane felt a chill go over him.

And then just as suddenly as it had appeared, the film faded away and the eyes were now clear and cold.

Kent sighed low.

He looked about the room and out to the night sky and then turned back to Shane.

The gun still held lightly in his hand.

He pointed the glinting barrel at the violin case.

"Open it and see how well I've taken care of your treasure."

Shane hesitated.

"Do it."

Shane went over to the case, knelt, and opened it.

The violin lay there against the soft velvet, the soft black velvet, gently gleaming.

A harsh yearning spread through him.

"Pick it up."

Shane put his trembling hands to the violin and then lifted it out of the case.

All the while Kent sat watching him.

A gentle look had come into the brown eyes.

The face had softened.

The gun now lay in his lap.

Shane put the violin to his shoulder.

Then his fingers touched the strings.

Tentatively.

Lovingly.

He lifted the bow from the case.

Suddenly he thought of Laurie in his arms and before he knew it he was playing chords.

Then snatches of melody.

He felt the tears well up inside of him and he stopped playing.

The night silence rushed into the room.

He heard the man's voice.

Soft and almost pleading.

"Play a selection, Lockwood. Anything you want. It will help you settle your frayed nerves."

And then he added quietly.

"And mine."

Shane looked over at him.

"You have no nerves," he said harshly.

"None?"

"That's right. No nerves and no heart."

75

Kent gazed at him and then smiled sadly.

His voice was low when he spoke.

"Ah, but I have. You almost forced me to kill you when you went for my throat. I did not want to do that. Not at all. You must believe that."

Shane was silent.

"Think about it, Lockwood. You would have choked the life out of me for a violin. Isn't that so?"

"I just wanted to get it and throw you out of here."

Kent shook his head.

"No."

"That's all I wanted."

Kent shook his head again.

"You are lying to yourself."

"I'm not."

"But you are. We both, when pushed to the wall, are killers."

"Killers?"

"Yes. We both are alike when you honestly and clearly think about it. Remember that always."

"Never," Shane said fiercely.

"But it is so, dear boy. I want something desperately and I will have nothing stand in my way. And you? . . ."

Shane didn't answer.

Kent laughed softly.

But his eyes were sad.

"I told you I'm a cultivated savage. And you? What do you think you'll find beneath your cultivated veneer? When pushed against the wall? What, Lockwood?"

Shane turned away from the sad, piercing eyes.

He didn't speak.

Then he heard the man say,

"Play. Please play. And then I'll leave."

Kent sat back in his seat and waited.

Shane slowly put the violin to his shoulder.

"Scarlatti?" Kent murmured.

And as the man said that, Shane thought of Elaine Stark and the night she had stopped him and praised his playing of the Scarlatti Variations.

What does she see in you, Kent?

What?

How did she ever get drawn into your life?

How?

The thoughts fled as he began to play.

Strangely, the difficult passage that he had trouble with during the concert became easy and flowing.

When he was done, he slowly put the violin back into the black case and handed it over to Kent.

Their eyes met.

"You'll get it back, Lockwood."

When I do what you want me to do, Shane thought bitterly.

Then he watched Kent go to the door, open it, and go out.

Now he was alone.

Alone with the dying night.

Chapter

15

He was sleeping a fitful sleep when he heard the door of the suite open quietly and then just as quietly close.

He sat up and through the misty darkness he saw a figure in white come closer and closer to him, and then he saw it was Laurie.

Her hair, blond and long, fell in a sweep.

Her face was pale.

Her eyes were large and staring.

"Laurie," he whispered.

"Shane."

She reached her hands to him and her fingertips were cold as ice.

"Laurie, what's the matter?"

"I'm scared. So very scared."

He just sat there unable to move.

He wanted to reach out and draw her to him.

But he couldn't.

She stood there staring at him and then suddenly she

turned and went slowly, slowly over to a chair and then sat down.

Staring at him.

Fear deep in her eyes.

Fear and longing.

He waited for her to speak.

When she did her voice was low and mournful.

"We are star-crossed lovers, Shane."

"No," he whispered.

She nodded and her blond hair swung about her.

"We are. We are. And we shall die. You and I."

"Laurie."

"Don't take me to the museum, Shane."

He stared speechlessly at her.

"Don't, Shane."

"How did you know I was going there?"

But she didn't answer.

"Don't do it, Shane. I don't want to see the tiara."

And then she got up from the chair and walked out to the terrace and stood there looking down at the pool.

She stood there, a white figure in a filmy nightgown.

She began to speak in that low, mournful voice.

Low.

So very low.

As if to herself.

But he could hear every word distinctly.

"Why did we ever meet? Why?"

He was silent.

"It's not fair. You say you care for me and yet you want to take me to see the tiara."

"Laurie, please listen to me."

"Leave the country. Let's leave together. Let them

have the violin. Is that so important? More important than your life?"

He didn't answer.

She came back to the threshold of the room.

And he thought of Juliet standing in her white nightgown, white against the fading night.

"More important than my life, Shane?"

"Nothing is more important than that."

"Are you sure?"

"Yes. Yes."

She shook her head slowly.

"You are lying to yourself, Shane. You are."

"I'm not."

She came slowly over to him.

Her white gown shimmered.

She was close and now he saw her clearly.

Her oval face pale in the darkness.

Her brown eyes had a golden tint.

Golden and gently glowing.

He felt his heart tremble as he gazed on her.

"You say you care for me and yet you would have me killed."

"No, Laurie. Never."

"You would," she said sadly.

Then she bent over and kissed him and he put his arms out to hold her close to him but she slipped away.

He saw her go to the door and open it.

"Laurie!" he cried out.

She stopped and turned to him.

A white, filmy figure.

Her voice floated through the darkness to him.

"Don't ask me to go, Shane. Please don't."

"Laurie!"

His voice rang out.

"Laurie, don't leave me alone."

But the door closed, blotting her out.

"Laurie," he whispered, his voice breaking.

And then he awoke and knew it was a dream.

Yet there were tears in his eyes.

Chapter

16

The morning sun was flowing into the room when the sound of the telephone woke him from his sleep.

He reached his hand out to the night table and picked up the receiver.

"Hello?"

"Shane?"

It was Laurie.

Her voice was bright and cheery.

"Oh."

"You sound sleepy."

"I am."

"It's past ten in the morning."

"I . . . I didn't sleep well."

"Why?"

"Just didn't."

"Thinking of me?"

"Yes," he said.

She laughed.

"I thought of you and I slept like a rock."

"Did you?"

"Uh-huh. What are you doing today?"

He hesitated and didn't speak.

"Want to spend some time with me, Shane?"

"Yes," he said.

"I want to do some sketching. Want to come along?"

"Sure."

"There's a statue I have to do. It's for one of my art teachers in New York."

"At NYU?"

"Yes. It's the Goldoni statue. You must have seen it by now. Everybody takes a look at it. I personally prefer the Colleoni statue, it has a lot of vigor and cold strength, a much better work of art. World famous. But that's what she wants me to work on. And that's what she's going to get."

He didn't speak.

"Shane?"

He still didn't speak.

"Are you there?"

"Yes, Laurie," he said.

"Well?"

"Well what?"

The day had suddenly become bleak to him.

"Want to go along?"

He didn't answer her.

"Shane?"

His hand was clammy on the phone.

He heard her voice again.

"What's with you this morning?"

"I'm okay," he said. "Just too sleepy, I guess."

"So? Are we on or not?"

He hesitated and then spoke.

"I'll come along."

"You sure?"

He nodded.

"Shane?"

"Yes, Laurie."

"Meet me in the lobby."

"All right."

"How about half an hour?"

"I'll be there, Laurie."

"Still thinking about last night?"

"What?"

"About you and me and last night?"

"Oh," he said.

"Shane, you're not with it today."

"I guess I'm not."

"Wake up, will you? Smell the coffee."

"Okay."

There was a slight pause and then he heard her voice again.

"Last night was very beautiful, wasn't it?"

"Yes, Laurie," he said.

Her voice became soft and tender.

"I can still feel your arms around me."

"Yes," he murmured.

"I like you very much, Shane."

"I do too, Laurie."

She suddenly laughed.

"You mean you love yourself very much or me?"

"I mean you, Laurie."

She laughed again.

"The lobby."

"Sure."

"Don't keep me waiting."

"I won't."

"Good-bye, Shane."

"Good-bye, Laurie."

But she didn't hang up.

"Venice at night is so enchanting, isn't it?"

And as she said that, he felt she was back in his arms again.

He didn't speak.

"Especially when you're with someone you like very much," she murmured.

"That is so," he said gently.

There was a pause.

"The lobby," she said.

And then he heard the click.

He lay there not moving.

A dark, bleak look was in his eyes.

Chapter
17

She kissed him when she came up to him in the lobby and when they were walking along the Grand Canal, the sun shining over her golden hair, she suddenly stopped and drew him close to her.

"I'll never forget last night, Shane. Will you?"

"No, Laurie."

"It left me breathless."

"I'll never forget it either, Laurie."

He held her and kissed her and then they drew apart and started walking again.

But within him, deep within, a chill lay.

And it didn't leave him as he stood by her, watching her sketch the Goldoni statue.

"How is it coming along, Shane?"

"Fine," he said.

"My heart's not in it."

He didn't say anything.

She stopped sketching and looked over at him.

"Shane?"

"Yes?"

"There's something wrong."

"What do you mean?"

"I feel it. I can't put my finger on it. But underneath it all . . ."

She stopped speaking and looked at him with a soft, pleading look.

It cut through him.

"Have I done something?" she asked.

"What?"

She reached over and touched his hand.

He felt himself quiver as she did that.

"I feel that I have, Shane. Please tell me."

He shook his head.

"No. Nothing's wrong, Laurie."

"Please be honest with me."

"I am."

"Is it one of your Irish moods?"

"What?"

"Is it, Shane?"

He laughed softly.

"I don't have any Irish moods, Laurie."

She suddenly began to laugh, too.

"Just what is an Irish mood?" she asked.

"I don't know."

"I don't either."

She touched his hand again.

"Then it's nothing?"

He nodded.

"Nothing."

She smiled gently and turned back to her sketching.

"Shane?"

"Yes?"

She didn't pause in her work.

Her eyes were on the statue and her hand was moving rapidly over the white sketch pad.

Overhead the sky was a pale Venetian blue.

The water in the canal sparkled like tiny waves of white silver under the late morning sun.

A gondola glided up close to them and the gondolier standing in the prow of the boat was tall and lean and had a tight, tanned face.

Brown eyes and a clipped mustache.

Shane trembled.

He could swear the man was Arthur Kent.

But he knew in his heart that it wasn't.

No one else was in the long, curved, black boat but the lean gondolier.

Shane stared at the man and heard Laurie speak.

"After I'm done sketching would you want to go with me?"

The gondolier and Shane were now facing each other for a fleeting instant.

He stared at Shane with a harsh, savage look in his large eyes.

Savage and murderous.

"Go where, Laurie?"

Then the man and the boat disappeared downstream into the fierce sunshine.

But the unsettling image remained.

Searing into Shane.

Laurie sketched in a few more lines on the white sheet and then spoke.

"Are you in the mood for a museum?"

He slowly, silently turned to her.

"What?"

His voice was low and hoarse.

"There is a small but lovely one not far from here."

He stood there taut and did not speak.

"It has a wonderful collection of rare diamonds. I love to go there."

She still had not turned from the statue.

"Would you like to come with me?"

He didn't answer.

"There's a tiara I always like to look at."

"Tiara?"

He barely murmured the word.

"Yes."

She continued sketching.

He stared at the figure standing before him in the glaring sunshine.

The back bent just a bit forward in concentration.

The blond, soft hair.

Flowing over her shoulders.

Glinting with iridescence.

And as he was staring at her, she suddenly turned about from the gleaming statue and faced him.

Her eyes upon him.

"Well?"

Her face was white and calm.

So very calm.

The golden eyes now clear and penetrating.

As if she could see through him to his dark secret.

As if she knew everything.

A tremor went through him.

No, he said.

It can't be.

It can't.

"Would you, Shane?"

He didn't answer.
She asked again.
He slowly nodded.
Then she smiled and turned back to her sketching.

Chapter

18

The instant he stood before the tiara he knew why Kent had wanted him to look at it. Its beauty was dazzling.

Almost overwhelming.

He saw again before him the man sitting in the darkened suite, his eyes glowing as he talked of the tiara.

The lean, tight face gone soft with desire.

Desire so intense and desperate.

The supple hand holding the gun.

He heard Laurie's voice.

"It's beautiful, isn't it, Shane?"

"Yes," he murmured.

"It just goes to my heart every time I see it."

"Does it?"

"Yes. Yes."

He felt her hand suddenly grasp his tightly.

Her lips trembled and opened slightly.

He looked at her.

Then within him, he said to himself, you want that tiara as much as he does, Laurie.

You do.

I can feel it within my very being.

I can.

And it sends a cold chill throughout me.

Cold.

So very cold.

You frighten me at this moment, Laurie.

You do.

"Yes, Laurie," he said quietly. "It is beautiful."

They stood there silent and alone.

Alone in a great stillness.

The tiara lay upon a stretch of black velvet in a case of thick glass.

The case stood in the center of the main room of the small museum.

There were but a few people in the one-story building at this morning hour.

A lone guard lounged in a shadowy corner of the room casually watching them and then letting his gaze wander away.

A ray of sunlight filtered through one of the dusty windows and settled onto the tiara.

It gave the diamonds a fiery glitter.

He heard Laurie softly gasp.

And for some strange reason, Shane thought of the diamond bracelet that Elaine Stark wore.

The glitter of its diamonds in the sea sunshine.

As she sat by him on Lido Beach.

Her shadow dark and long on the white sand.

He turned back to Laurie.

She was staring at the fiery diamonds.

Her eyes had become large and more golden.

Her face flushed red.

He felt her hand hot against his.

"Byron was so much in love with Teresa Guiccioli," she said.

Her voice lowered, almost to a whisper.

"He had the tiara made especially for her. She wore it whenever they went out to one of the elegant balls in Venice."

She pressed his hand again and smiled almost wistfully.

"They were quite a pair. No one like them in the world."

He kept looking at her.

"Can you imagine them walking into one of the white palaces on the Grand Canal and all the aristocrats at the ball freezing into silence? As if a god and a goddess had suddenly come down and stood before them?"

With her wearing the tiara, he thought.

Laurie spoke again.

"Teresa was so very beautiful. And he was so handsome. Like you, Shane."

"Cut it," he said gently.

She smiled and then pointed to a small glass case near them.

"A famous artist painted a miniature of her. Byron ordered it. It's in that case."

"The Guiccioli Miniature."

"You've heard of it?"

She seemed pleased.

"Yes, Laurie."

"Did you ever see it before?"

"No. This will be the first time."

"I saw it first in New York. At the Met. But I was alone then."

She pressed his hand.

"And the tiara, Laurie?"

She shook her head.

"They didn't have it there. It's never been allowed outside this museum."

"It's their treasure," he said.

"It is."

And a poignant look came into his gray eyes.

"What is it, Shane?"

But he was thinking of the Guarnerius.

How cruel it is to steal one's treasure.

She drew him over to the small case.

He stood there gazing at the tiny masterpiece.

At the large brown eyes, almost golden, the light brown hair, almost blond, and the shapely oval face.

It startled him.

She was aware of this.

"What's the matter, Shane?"

He turned to her.

His eyes studying her.

"What, Shane?"

He finally spoke.

"She looks so much like you, Laurie."

"Do you think so?"

"Very much. It could almost be a miniature of you."

She smiled.

"No."

"Aren't you aware of it?"

She shrugged.

"Some resemblance, but that's all."

"If the hair were just a bit more blond and the . . ."

He didn't finish.

He thought her face had become pale.

94

She abruptly turned away from the case.

"Let's go, Shane. Out into the sunshine again. I have to finish my sketch."

"All right."

"Just a few more touches."

"Sure."

But she paused to look at the tiara again.

The fire still lay in the diamonds.

It set her eyes glowing again.

The golden eyes.

And looking at her, he thought of the miniature.

There is a line from Teresa to you.

There is.

There must be.

And you know it.

You do.

"Laurie."

She looked up at him.

"Yes?"

"Tell me."

And he stopped.

"What, Shane?"

"What happened to them?"

"To Byron and Teresa?"

"Yes."

"Why do you want to know?"

"Just tell me."

She hesitated before speaking.

"It ended . . . tragically."

"How?"

"I guess . . . their love just died."

He didn't say anything.

She moved closer to him.

"Love dies if you let it. Isn't that so, Shane?"

"Yes, Laurie," he said. "If you let it."

But the fear was still in her eyes.

Shane put his large hand out to her small one and held it tight.

Then they left the museum.

Chapter
19

He was lying in bed looking out the window at the bright, moonlit sky and thinking of the day he had just spent with Laurie.

On the night table a little glass figurine of a delicately prancing horse gleamed softly.

He glanced at the glass horse and smiled almost wistfully.

Then he reached out and picked it up.

Gently.

The touch of it stirred him to his heart.

For it made him see Laurie standing in the little glassware shop, buying the figurine and then turning and giving it to him.

"No, Laurie."

"Please."

"But . . ."

"Just to remember me by, Shane."

"I'll remember you," he said.

"You sure?"

"Yes."

"Even when you're old?"

"Even then."

She laughed and they went out of the shop.

Even then, Laurie.

A ray of moonlight stole into the room and touched the small glass head of the horse.

The glass became iridescent.

He kept looking at it.

Even then, Laurie.

Then he slowly, carefully put the figurine back in its place.

He lay back in bed, his eyes half-closed, and he thought of Murano.

"Let's go to Murano, Shane."

"The island?"

"Yes. It's famous for its glassware."

"Okay with me."

As the *motoscafo* sped over the pale blue water on its way to the island, he watched the wind ripple through Laurie's blond hair.

The sky above them was cloudless.

He kept looking at her hair glinting in the strong overhead sun.

The clean, fine profile.

The large, golden eyes staring ahead over the open water.

I shall never forget you, he said to himself.

Never.

You are becoming part of me.

"You are," he said.

He spoke but his voice was low.

Yet she heard him.

For she turned to him.

"What did you say, Shane?"

He shook his head.

"Nothing, Laurie."

She put her hand to her straying strands of hair and smiled.

"Happy?"

"Yes."

"Very?"

"And you?"

"Very," she said.

"I am, too."

She leaned to him and kissed him.

"Laurie," he whispered.

"Shane."

Then she kissed him again and turned back to the sea.

He stood there watching her, still feeling the touch of her lips on his.

A sad look came into his gray eyes.

His heart was heavy.

I feel that I will lose you, he said to himself.

And maybe my life, too.

We're star-crossed lovers, Laurie.

He gazed at the stretch of blue water.

I'm caught in a current and I don't know where it's taking me.

I don't.

And there's nothing I can do about it.

Nothing.

The boat slowed down and then the motor was cut off.

Only the sound of the rippling water remained.

The boat glided silently to its dock.

"We're here," she said softly.

"Yes, Laurie."

They got out of the boat and then walked along the dock and onto the sunny path.

He took her hand and they began to stroll along, content with each other.

"Let's go into one of the glass factories, Shane."

He nodded.

"Anything you want, Laurie."

"Anything?"

"Uh-huh."

She looked at him.

A dancing, merry look in her eyes.

"How about some money?"

"Money?"

"You must have a lot put away by now. From your years of concerts."

"I have some. How much do you want?"

"Nothing."

And they both laughed and went into one of the factory buildings.

Later on, he would think of that.

Later on.

And he would wonder how important money was to her.

What would she do to get it?

But that was later on.

"Fascinating, isn't it, Shane?"

"Yes."

They stood close to each other and watched the glass-blowers at work.

"Venetian glass has been famous for a long time," she said.

She pointed to a worker fashioning a glass dolphin.

"His craft goes back hundreds of years. During the sixteenth century those secrets were fiercely guarded. Then Venetian glassmaking was at its peak."

They watched the dolphin slowly taking its final shape.

"If a master craftsman left Venice and then revealed his secrets he was followed and generally caught and brought back to be sentenced."

"To what?"

A strange look came into her eyes.

"His hands were cut off."

He stared at her speechlessly.

"That's true, Shane. Quite true. Venice could be a very cruel place."

Yes, he thought.

Yes, it can.

He lay on the bed staring at the figurine and then he thought of Lido Beach.

They had gone there just before sunset.

The sea was calm.

The long, low waves were rose-streaked.

A huge silence was over everything.

They walked till they came to a desolate spot and sat down and just gazed quietly at the fading horizon.

Then he turned and took her in his arms.

Soon night came flooding over them.

And they lost themselves in its depth.

* * *

The moonlight glimmered over the little figurine and it was then that the phone rang.

A cold, startling ring.

He lay there unmoving.

Letting the phone ring.

Then it stopped.

The silence came back into the room.

And soon the phone began its ring again.

He reached over and picked it up.

"Hello?"

"I know you're there."

"Yes. You know everything. Don't you?"

The soft laugh.

"Lockwood."

"Yes?"

"Tomorrow is Saturday."

"And?"

"I want to see you."

Shane didn't speak.

"Meet me at the Piazza San Marco."

"When?"

"Twelve o'clock. We'll have lunch together."

"I don't care to have lunch with you."

The soft laugh.

"Then we'll have a drink together."

Shane was silent.

"Tomorrow."

Tomorrow is Saturday, Shane thought.

And after Saturday always comes Sunday.

He heard the click of the phone.

Chapter

20

He was walking along one of the sunlit alleys on his way to the square when he heard a voice.

"Shane Lockwood."

He turned and saw Elaine Stark.

She came up to him.

"I must speak to you."

He looked at her strained, white face.

The dark, brooding eyes.

"Before you see him."

"All right."

She glanced quickly about and then pointed to a small hotel that stood in a shadowy corner of the alley.

Beyond it was the gleaming water of a canal.

"Let's go in there," she said.

He followed her into the small lobby and over to a couch and chairs.

The place was almost empty.

The sun filtered through a tall window and onto a dusty carpet.

A lean, gray-haired clerk stood behind a desk sorting mail.

He glanced up at them and then went back to his work.

Shane waited for her to speak.

She put her hand out to his, touched it, and then drew it away.

"You're going to meet him in the square, aren't you?"

He nodded.

"Yes," she sighed softly.

She looked down for an instant at the diamonds glittering faintly on her slender wrist.

And a fleeting thought came to him.

How much did those diamonds cost?

What was the price?

Who paid with his blood for them?

She looked up and their eyes met.

And he felt that she had read his thought, for she flinched.

Her hands trembled slightly.

Then she spoke.

"He's accomplished what he planned."

"What do you mean?"

"The first phase. It's done."

He was silent.

"Last night."

"And now?"

But she didn't answer him.

"You're leaving tomorrow for home."

"Yes."

"Don't take the girl with you."

"Laurie?"

"Yes."

He stared at her.

"She's going to ask you to get a flight for her. With you."

"No."

"Don't do it."

"How do you know she will?"

A poignant, lost look came into the woman's eyes.

"Because I know."

He didn't speak.

"She cares an awful lot for you. Doesn't she?"

She does, he thought.

I know she does.

And I for her.

"You promised me that you would not draw her into this. Do you remember?"

"But . . ."

"She's in."

"What do you mean?"

Elaine Stark rose from her seat.

"Don't take her with you."

Then she turned and left him.

At the desk, the lean clerk looked up from his mail and over to Shane.

His face was taut and grim.

But in his eyes was dark pity.

As if he knew Shane's fate.

Chapter

21

Shane watched him approach the table. He was wearing a white polo shirt, open at the collar, and a pair of yellow slacks.

Pale yellow.

The sun was on him.

And Shane thought of Richard Cory.

Who glittered when he walked.

Kent smiled as he sat down.

"You're on time, Lockwood."

Shane sat back in his chair and didn't speak.

"Changed your mind about lunch?"

Shane shook his head.

"No."

"Not hungry?"

"I am. But I'd rather eat alone."

"You despise me."

"That would be putting it mildly."

Kent laughed.

"But you also fear me."

"Yes."

"Why?"

"Because you're a savage. And one never knows what a savage will do."

"That's true."

He motioned to a waiter.

"A cultivated savage. That means there's a subtle mind at work. A mind hard to beat."

The waiter came over.

Kent turned to Shane.

"Do you mind if I eat?"

"Go ahead."

"You're not drinking?"

"No."

"Just sitting."

"That's right."

Kent ordered in his flawless Italian and the waiter went off.

"You know," Shane said, "when you came up to me I thought of a poem."

"Which one?"

"That one by Edwin Arlington Robinson. Most schoolboys learn it. At one time or another. I'm sure you did."

" 'Richard Cory'?"

"That's it."

"And?"

"He glittered when he walked."

Kent smiled.

"Nice of you to think of me that way."

"At the end of the poem . . ."

"Yes?"

"Richard Cory puts a bullet through his head."

Kent laughed, but his face had paled.

"And you think that's how I will end?"

"One way or another, a bullet will go through your head," Shane said quietly, and his gray eyes were cold.

"It hasn't happened yet."

"It will."

"You read too many poems, Lockwood. In life, the villains always die in bed."

Shane didn't speak.

The waiter came over with a glass of amber wine.

He glanced at Shane and then walked away.

"In bed, Lockwood. Either on their Southampton estates or in their Park Avenue apartments. But in bed."

He lifted the glass and sipped the wine and then set the glass down on the table.

The wine sparkled in the sun.

"And in the morning the newspapers print glowing obituaries. Isn't that so, dear boy?"

Shane looked away from him to the pigeons, ever rising and settling in the square.

And then to the glowing campanile.

And as he looked at it he thought of the Bridge of Sighs where the convicted ones walked their mournful way to the dungeons to rot their lives out.

Many of them innocent.

Sent there centuries ago by villains.

Villains.

He's right.

I read too many poems.

He heard Kent's soft voice.

"Did the tiara impress you?"

Shane turned back to the man.

"Did it, Lockwood?"

Shane slowly nodded.

"I thought it would."

"It's very beautiful," Shane said.

Kent shook his head.

"Beautiful is not the word. It's incomparable. Only one of its kind in the entire world. Believe me, I know. I know."

He paused and then went on.

In the same, almost breathless, voice.

"I've desired it for many years. Do you hear me? Many years."

Shane stared at him.

A cold thrill of fear spreading through his being.

For the brown eyes glowed with the fire in them.

The lean face had become taut and the bone structure beneath the tan skin seemed to show.

As if Shane were looking at the skull beneath the face.

The voice of the man came to him as from a distance.

"It presented so many problems. Each one had to be solved."

A long, supple forefinger tapped on the glass table.

"Each one."

Tapped again.

Then it stopped and the man spoke.

"Only a master could do it. A master. Do you hear me, Lockwood? Do you? A master."

His voice rose and then suddenly the man leaned back in his chair and abruptly stopped speaking.

The tension swiftly left the face.

A sardonic smile came into the eyes.

Kent was now in complete control of himself.

At ease.

He slowly raised the glass and drained the wine.

He dried his thin lips with his white napkin.

All the while Shane looked at the man.

I've come to hate you, he thought to himself.

Hate you bitterly.

And then he said to himself, We hate those who hold us in their power.

It's always been that way.

Down through history.

And you hold me now.

Don't you?

The waiter came over with the appetizer and Kent smiled appreciatively at him.

"Grazie."

Then he ate slowly, delicately, and didn't speak to Shane.

Above them, the Venetian sky was blue and serene.

The campanile shone brightly in the pure sun.

Kent finished eating and then put the plate aside.

"The food is always good here. Don't you think?"

Shane didn't answer.

"Always good. The tiara is no longer in the glass case, Lockwood."

"What?"

"Someone took it during the night."

Shane was silent.

"So the problem is now solved."

"There was nothing in the newspapers or on television," Shane said.

"I know."

"Why?"

Kent laughed softly.

110

"The museum will simply announce that it has lent the tiara for an exhibition in another country."

"I don't believe you."

"You should. It's all because of the insurance policy. A very heavy one. The company will pay a very generous sum to the thief or thieves to get the tiara back."

He smiled.

"This is par for the course. It's been done before, believe me. Museums throughout the world have had their share of thefts. And never a word about them. I know, Lockwood. I know."

I believe you now, Shane thought.

A bleak feeling spread within him.

He heard Kent speak again.

A strange, almost fierce look came into his eyes.

He leaned forward to Shane and tapped with his forefinger on the glass of the table.

"But it won't be done that way this time."

He shook his head grimly.

"No. Not this time."

He tapped again on the glass.

His eyes almost on fire.

"This time the thief wants it for himself."

He paused to catch his breath and then went on.

"To enjoy it on a winter's night when the snow is on the ground and the wind is blowing, a cold, cold wind. Then he will sit in his Park Avenue apartment and go to his vault and take the tiara out and set it in front of him. And just look at it and enjoy it."

He leaned back in his chair and sighed softly.

"To enjoy it, Lockwood."

He took out a cigarette, lit it, and smoked.

His face became calm.

The eyes clear and penetrating.

Kent began to speak again.

In a low, meditative voice.

Almost as if to himself.

"The Spanish have a saying: Each to his own madness. That is my madness. I'm fully aware of it. What is yours?"

Shane looked away from him to the campanile.

"It's your precious violin. Your divine playing. Without them, you will slowly die. The same as those poor wretches who hung in the cages up there, centuries ago. We have always been cruel to each other, Lockwood. Always. It will never change."

He smiled almost sadly at Shane.

"I can see in your eyes that you agree with me."

Maybe I do, Shane thought.

"You'll grow older and wiser. And become cynical."

Will I grow older?

And Kent seemed to read his thoughts.

"Just do as I want you to do. And you'll grow older."

He rose from his seat and looked down at Shane.

"Tomorrow you board the plane. You will be carrying your violin case."

He took out money from his wallet and set it on the table.

"Please pay the waiter for me."

Then he turned and walked away from Shane.

And looking at him glittering in the sun, Shane thought of Richard Cory.

Who will get the bullet in his head?

You or I?
For that is the way it will surely end.
The only way.

Chapter

22

He was drawn back to the museum, as if by some strange, magnetic force that he couldn't resist.

And now he stood before the empty glass case.

Staring at the desolate stretch of black velvet.

Reading the stark white card.

The Guiccioli Tiara is now on loan to an exhibition in Bern, Switzerland.

Bern.

That's as good a city as any, he thought sardonically.

But it will never go there.

Not in this century.

It's going to New York.

As sure as there's a hell in this world, it's going to New York.

To a luxurious Park Avenue apartment.

Never to come back.

Never.

And there is a hell in this world.

There is.

And there are devils still around.

Cultivated, savage devils.

He clenched his big hands into fists.

Then he turned away from the black velvet and went over slowly to look at the Guiccioli Miniature.

He stood there in the museum silence and an awful sadness swept over him.

The pain lay deep in his gray eyes.

"Teresa," he whispered.

Teresa Guiccioli and Lord Byron.

They loved each other so desperately.

The tiara was an absolute expression of his love for her.

Love.

Deep and eternal.

And yet it ended so tragically.

Ended.

Finished.

La commedia è finita.

All tragedies become comedies in the end.

Don't they?

He stood there gazing at the hauntingly beautiful face in the miniature and he felt the tears about to come to his eyes.

It was then that he heard the voice.

Soft and appealing.

"Shane."

He turned and saw Laurie standing near him.

Her eyes were large and sad.

Her blond hair was drawn back and now she looked exactly like Teresa.

Exactly.

"We were supposed to have lunch," she said.

He didn't speak.

"At the trattoria close to the hotel. At one."

You are Teresa, he thought.

"I saw you passing the hotel and I called to you but you didn't seem to hear me. You just walked on."

"I forgot," he said.

"I followed you. Here."

"I'm sorry."

She put out her hand to him.

"What is it, Shane?"

You are Teresa.

Come to life.

"There's something wrong, Shane. There is."

"Nothing," he said.

"There must be. Could you tell me?"

He shook his head silently.

"Why did you come back here, Shane?"

"To see the tiara."

"Oh."

"It's gone," he said.

"Yes. It is."

He watched her as she gazed at the empty case.

Her face had paled just a bit.

But it was calm.

Her hands at her sides.

Unmoving.

"You don't seem surprised, Laurie," he said quietly.

She was silent.

Still looking at the bleak, empty case.

"I thought you would be," he said.

She turned to him.

"Why?"

116

"You said they never let the tiara out of the museum."

Her large, golden eyes looked into his.

"Did I?"

"Yes, Laurie."

She shrugged.

"Well, I guess they broke the rule this time."

"They did," he said.

"Must have a very good reason."

"Yes. I'm sure they had."

His voice had become cold and hard.

She flinched and he saw fear come into her eyes.

Her hands began to tremble.

"Shane."

"Yes."

"Shane, what's wrong?"

"I told you. Nothing."

"It's something I did. Tell me."

He looked away from her to the guard lounging in the corner.

The man's face was in shadow.

Are you in with them? Shane asked.

Are you?

And she, standing next to me, is she, too?

In this corrupt, greedy world of ours?

"Shane?"

He turned back to her.

"I feel cold in here," she said.

You should, he thought grimly.

"Let's go out into the sunlight."

He still stood there.

"Please, Shane."

She put her hand into his.

117

And he felt a rush of feeling for her.
I love you so much, Laurie.
Don't break my heart.
"Let's go, Shane."
Then they went out of the museum.

Chapter
23

They didn't speak to each other till they came to the Goldoni statue. Then she turned to him and spoke in a low and anguished voice.

"What is it, Shane? Why do you treat me so cruelly?"

"Cruelly?"

"Yes. You look at me so coldly. There is suspicion in your eyes. You just walk along saying nothing."

"It's one of my moods," he said.

She shook her head and her hair glinted in the strong sun.

"No. It's not. I know something is wrong."

He felt the hurt that was within her.

But he didn't speak.

"Last night at Lido you held me in your arms and you said . . . you said . . ."

Her voice almost broke.

He saw the hint of tears in her eyes.

I said I loved you, Laurie.

Yes, I said that.

And it came from my heart.

He heard her speak again.

"And now? Now you treat me as if you hate me."

"I don't, Laurie. Not that."

"You do."

He couldn't bear the expression on her face.

There was so much pain in it.

He looked away to the statue and remembered her standing in the sun, her shoulders hunched forward just a bit, concentrating on her sketch. He knew he would never forget that figure and the white pad in its hand.

That slender, graceful white hand.

"You just don't tell me the truth," he blurted out.

"What?"

"Truth."

"What do you mean?"

He hesitated and then spoke.

"For starters. You say you're Irish on one side of your family."

"I am."

"And the other?"

She flushed and was silent.

"Well?"

"Why do you want to know?"

"Just want to."

"Italian."

"I thought so," he said grimly.

The color was now high in her oval face.

"What's wrong with being Italian?"

"The name, Laurie."

"Why?"

"Because it's important to me."

"Why is it important?"

"Just tell me."

"Guiccioli."

"I thought so," he said.

"I'm her last living descendant."

"Living?"

"Yes."

"What about your mother?"

"She had Teresa's name. She died when I was a small child. I have a stepmother."

"The one with the big house in Baltimore?"

She nodded.

He looked away from her to the sparkling water of the canal.

"The tiara," he said.

"What about it?"

He turned back to her.

"You feel the tiara really belongs to you, that you should have inherited it. Isn't that so?"

Her eyes flashed.

"Isn't that so, Laurie?"

When she spoke, her voice was low and cutting.

"It does. Nobody had the right to give it away."

"What do you mean?"

"It was being handed down in the family and then somebody gave it away. It should have been mine. *Mine*, Shane."

Her voice rose and echoed over the water.

"It belongs to me."

"And now you want it back. Don't you?"

She didn't answer him.

"Do you know an Arthur Kent?"

"Kent?"

"Yes."

His eyes bored into her.

He thought she had paled.

But she shook her head.

"No. Why should I?"

He sighed softly.

"Just a thought, Laurie."

She put her hand out desperately to his and then held it tightly.

He trembled within.

"Shane."

"Yes?"

"There is something terribly wrong. What is it?"

"Nothing, Laurie."

"I'm scared."

"Scared of what, Laurie?"

Her eyes looked fearfully into his.

"Of losing you," she said.

He didn't speak.

But within him he said, I'm beginning to hate the tiara.

With a desolate hatred.

Chapter

24

The sunlight filtered through leaves of the small trees and onto Laurie and Shane.

Light and shadow played over the white tablecloth.

She put down her espresso cup and smiled faintly at him.

They had spoken very little during the meal.

Underneath it all was a tension.

Something is happening to us, Laurie, he thought.

Something is tearing us apart.

"Shane."

"Yes?"

"You're leaving tomorrow, aren't you?"

He nodded.

"What plane are you taking?"

"The two o'clock."

"Is it all booked?"

"I should think so at this time of the year."

She sipped the espresso and then spoke again.

There were flecks of shadow on the oval face.

The eyes were large and golden.

"You always book an extra seat for your violin, don't you?"

"Yes."

He waited.

"Could you give me that seat?"

"What?" he said softly.

"I'll manage with the violin on my lap."

"Laurie."

"Shane, I'll feel so awfully alone with you gone. It would just be . . . be . . ."

Her voice trailed off into the silence.

He looked at her and thought of Elaine Stark's words to him.

She'll ask you to take her along.

Don't, Shane.

"Please?"

"But you planned to stay here another week."

"I know I did."

"And now?"

"I just told you I want to go home."

He was silent.

She leaned forward to him.

"We could see each other in New York. Walk the streets of the Village. Sit in Washington Square. We . . . Shane . . ."

She stopped speaking.

Her eyes looked pleadingly into his.

"Let me think," he said.

"I just want to sit next to you."

He picked his cup up and then set it down again.

"Laurie."

"Yes?"

"How did you know I always book an extra seat?"

"How?"

"Yes."

She faltered and then spoke.

"I . . . I read it in one of the articles about you."

"Oh."

"Well? Will you do it?"

He didn't answer her.

"Don't you want me along?"

"I never said that, Laurie."

"Then what is it?"

"Stop hassling me," he said sharply.

She flinched and drew away.

"I'm sorry Shane. I didn't mean to."

His voice was softer when he spoke again.

"I'm under a little tension, Laurie."

He rose.

"Let's get out into the sun."

"We are in the sun."

"Let's get out anyway."

She smiled wanly at him, and they left the restaurant.

Chapter
25

But when they were sitting on Lido Beach watching the fiery sun slowly, slowly drop into the wide sea, its flame quickly extinguished, only then, when darkness was coming in over them, did she ask him again.

Now his arms were about her.

Her fragrance hovering over him.

And it was then that he said he would take her.

It was then.

Chapter

26

He was sitting on the terrace of his suite gazing at the moonless sky and thinking of Laurie when he heard the lock of the door softly click and the knob slowly turn.

The door opened silently.

A thin, cold ray of light came into the room.

The door closed and the ray was gone.

"Lockwood?"

He saw the lean figure of Arthur Kent standing in the room.

Then the lamp was turned on and he saw the man clearly.

He was carrying the black violin case.

Shane came into the room and stood there looking at the man and the case.

"You'll carry this onto the plane tomorrow," Kent said.

He set the case on the table and then slowly opened it.

"Come over."

Shane felt a quiver in his heart as he looked down at the Guarnerius.

The violin glowed softly.

"You have the same look in your eyes as I must have when I look at the treasured tiara," Kent said gently.

Shane didn't move.

"We are alike. I told you that, Lockwood."

Shane put his hand tentatively on the violin and the instant his fingers touched the glowing wood, he knew it was not the Guarnerius.

A cold wave of anger swept over him.

He turned bitterly to Kent.

"This is a fake," he said harshly.

Kent smiled.

"It is. But a masterful one. Don't you think?"

Shane stood there, his hands clenched.

He heard Kent's low, maddening voice.

"The craftsman needed another couple of days to finish it. That is why I had you change your flight from Friday to Sunday."

He smiled.

"It's a perfect copy. Don't you think?"

Shane didn't speak.

"The tiara is inside the violin. Secure. Very secure. You'll take it through customs and into the United States for me."

Shane felt a cold sweat break out over him.

He heard Kent's voice again.

"You're a celebrity. You probably won't be stopped. But if you are, you'll open the case and show them the Guarnerius and they'll smile and pass you through. Simple, isn't it?"

He laughed gently and spoke again.

"You'll do that for me. Won't you, dear boy?"

And Shane's control broke.

He began to shout.

"Damn you! I've had enough. *Enough!*"

He grabbed the violin out of the case and raised it high, about to bring it down and smash it on the table, when he heard Kent's sharp voice.

"Don't. Or I'll put a bullet through your heart."

The gun gleamed in his tight hand.

The lean face was grim and taut.

The eyes fierce and savage.

Shane breathed a sigh and then slowly put the violin back into the case.

The two stood looking at each other.

Then Kent called out in a low and penetrating voice.

"Mario."

The door opened and a man in a white suit, with black hair, smoothed down, came into the room.

The face was a harsh one.

The expression impassive.

And Shane saw again the man who stood on the Rialto Bridge watching Laurie sketch.

The door closed silently.

Kent stared with a cold and intent expression at Shane.

"I think it's high time you've had your object lesson," he said. "I thought we would have no need for it. But I see now it's very necessary."

He turned and curtly nodded to the man.

The man came over close to Shane and opened his jacket and took out a knife that was tucked in his belt.

The blade was long and slender.

It shone in the lamplight.

129

Shane stood there staring at the two men.

"Sit down, Lockwood," Kent commanded.

Shane did not move.

"Do as I say."

"What do you want?"

"To teach you a little lesson."

There was a soft, squirting sound from the barrel of the gun and Shane felt the singe of the bullet as it skimmed his hair and landed in the wall behind him.

"Well, Lockwood?"

Shane slowly sat down in the chair.

"Put out one of your hands."

"What?"

"Do as I say."

Kent raised the glinting barrel of the gun and pointed it at Shane.

Shane slowly, fearfully extended his right hand.

Kent grimly shook his head.

"The left. The one you use to finger the strings."

"No," Shane said and began to rise.

"Do it."

"Never."

Kent leaned forward and hit Shane with the butt of his gun.

Shane staggered and then fell back into the chair.

His eyes had a dull, hopeless look in them.

"The hand," Kent said in a low and fierce voice.

Shane didn't move.

Kent reached forward and pulled Shane's hand onto the table.

"Just the palm," he said to Mario. "Just that."

The man made a quick slit in the palm of Shane's

hand and the blood started to trickle out and onto the table.

"Enough, Mario."

The man nodded silently and drew away.

Then Kent took out a white handkerchief and tied it over the palm.

"The next time you act up it will be a finger. One of your precious fingers, Lockwood. Is that clear to you?"

Shane didn't answer.

Kent went over to the case and closed it.

Then he silently handed it to Mario.

All the time Shane sat there staring with despair at the two men.

He heard Kent's voice as through a mist.

"The violin case will be in the hotel vault. You'll pick it up tomorrow and then go to the plane."

He paused and then went on.

"You'll be watched. Every minute. Remember that, Lockwood."

He went to the door.

Mario silently at his side.

You're like two sleek, savage animals, Shane thought bitterly.

And I'm caught in your jungle.

The door closed.

Chapter

27

He was sitting up in bed, just staring into the bleak darkness, when the phone rang.

He picked it up.

"Hello?"

"Shane?"

It was Elaine Stark's voice.

"Yes?"

"I was able to get this call through. He won't know about it. I have to talk to you. Listen to me. I've but a few minutes before he comes back."

Shane waited.

"Did he hurt you?"

"No. I'm all right."

"You should watch out. Every move you make. Don't cross him. Please, Shane. Please, for your sake. You don't know him as I do."

"I know him," Shane said coldly.

"You don't. He's very capable of killing me. Without

a word. If he found out that I made this call, he . . . he would . . ."

She didn't go on.

"Elaine," he said.

And his heart went out to her.

"When you go back to the States, don't contact the police. He'll get to you before you do it. And even if you do it, he'll get to you. I tell you I know. I know. From the past. No one has ever beaten him. Not for years, Shane. No one. Don't try."

"Why do you stay with him?"

"Why does the girl want to go with you?"

He didn't answer.

"Because she loves you, Shane."

Her voice almost broke when she said that.

And you love him, Shane thought sadly.

No matter what he is.

Or what he does.

You're caught, as I am.

You love him.

And love gets into your being and stays there.

Never to leave.

I know, Elaine.

How well I know.

Her voice came through to him.

"Shane, don't take her with you. You're only drawing her into this. He doesn't trust you with her. He feels you've become too involved with her. That you'll tell her things and he might have to kill her. Can you understand that? Can you?"

"Yes," Shane said softly.

"Break off with her."

"What?" he whispered.

"Shane."

He didn't speak.

"Do you hear me?"

He still couldn't speak.

"Until this is over. You must do that. For her."

"I would lose Laurie for good if I did that."

"You must take the chance."

"Lose her," he said again.

"There's no other way. Would you want Laurie to die?"

He was about to speak when he heard her voice cut in.

"He's back. I didn't hear him come in."

"Elaine."

But he heard the click.

And then he sat there, looking into the overwhelming darkness.

Chapter

28

"Why?"

The one word she said cut into him.

He sat there looking across the table at her.

Her face had become pale.

Deathly pale.

"I . . . I just can't, Laurie."

"But last night you said you would take me. You promised me, Shane."

"I know."

"I was looking forward to it. So much, Shane. You have no idea how much."

"I know," he said again.

She leaned forward to him.

"What has happened since? What?"

They were sitting in the square and before them the campanile rose into a cloudless sky.

The pigeons were settling and fluttering and all was the same.

And all is not the same, he said to himself forlornly.

Even the sun is not the same.

It glares cruelly into my eyes.

And into hers.

I can almost see the tears deep, deep within them, ready to appear.

"Tell me, Shane. You must."

He looked away from her and began to speak.

He couldn't bear to see her pain.

"I . . . I've been doing a lot of thinking, Laurie."

"About what?"

"About us."

"What about us?"

He turned back to her.

"I think we've been going too fast."

She flinched and pulled away from him.

Her mouth dropped open.

He felt as if he had slapped her.

He could almost see the impress of his hand on her white face.

"What do you mean?"

It was hard for him to speak.

"We ought to draw back and . . ."

He stopped.

"And what?"

He waited and then spoke again.

Her large, golden eyes ever upon him.

"Not see each other for a while."

"For a while?"

He silently nodded.

"Why not forever?"

"Laurie."

She was now standing, looking down at him.

The tears were now in her eyes.

136

Her lips trembled.

But her voice was steady when she spoke.

You look so beautiful now, he thought.

So breathtakingly beautiful.

Don't leave me, Laurie.

Please don't.

"I will forget I ever met you, Shane. Ever."

Then she turned and walked away from him.

The sun harshly glinting on her golden hair.

He sat there motionless.

I feel numb now, he said to himself.

Because it all happened so quickly.

It was over before I knew it.

But soon the pain will begin.

And it will settle deep within me.

Never to go away.

Never.

Chapter

29

The manager took the violin case out of the vault and handed it to Shane.

"I do hope your stay with us was a very pleasant one, Mr. Lockwood."

"It was."

The man smiled.

"Always an honor to have a virtuoso like you as our guest. Please come back as soon as possible."

Their eyes met.

Then Shane turned and walked away from the man.

Out of the hotel and into the sun.

Mario silently at his side.

And Mario was with him when they boarded the *motoscafo* to take them to the airport at Mestre.

And he was at his side when they got out of the boat and stood on the dock.

Shane waited till the rest of the passengers were gone.

He stood there looking out at the blue, rippling water.

His gray eyes cold and hard.

His lips thin.

Then he turned to Mario.

"I guess this is where we say good-bye."

The man nodded silently.

Shane set the case on the dock.

"Mario," he said, and smiled.

"Yes?"

And it was then that Shane hit him hard in the stomach, and as the man doubled up he hit him again, this time solidly on the jaw, and the man sank down to the dock.

The blood trickling from his lips.

A dazed look in the black eyes.

"Just to remember me by, Mario."

Then Shane picked up the black violin case and walked into the airport building.

I could have broken my hand on that hard jaw, Shane thought.

But it would've been worth it.

Yes.

Then he went to the counter and checked in.

As he was about to enter the boarding area, he felt a man close to him.

"That was a mistake. A bad mistake."

And the man was gone.

Chapter

30

He looked through the small window and out into the coming night. The sound of the plane ever in his being.

Then he saw almost to the horizon the glitter of the last of the sun.

And it suddenly seemed to him to be the glitter of diamonds.

The diamonds of the tiara.

Glittering.

Ever glittering.

And then the sun flamed its last glow and the diamonds seemed to him to be dripping with blood.

And it was then that he said to himself, It shall end in blood.

It has to.

He turned away from the window and bowed his head.

Chapter

31

"Would you open the case?"

Shane paled.

He was in Kennedy Airport going through customs.

He stared at the inspector.

What's going to happen now?

My luggage wasn't even touched.

Not even looked at.

And now he wants to . . .

Shane heard the man's voice again.

He had piercing brown eyes.

The man knows, Shane thought desperately.

Somehow he knows.

He was tipped off.

They often are.

"Mr. Lockwood?"

Someone has betrayed Arthur Kent.

Shane slowly opened the case and then stood back and watched the man.

This could be where it all ends, he thought grimly.

I don't want it to end this way.

All I want now is to get the Guarnerius back and never see or hear of Arthur Kent again.

Not as long as I live.

Maybe in hell I'll meet him.

Maybe there.

For bringing the tiara to him.

In a way I'm just as guilty as he is.

But I was caught.

And there was no way out.

"That's not a Strad, is it?"

"No," Shane said. "It's a Guarnerius."

"Ah," the man sighed.

Shane felt a chill go through him as the inspector carefully, devotedly, lifted the violin from the case.

It shone in the hard overhead lights.

Shane trembled as the inspector examined the violin.

His hand gently, carefully feeling the wood and outlines of the instrument.

His eyes ever piercing.

Then he heard the voice.

It was low.

Very low.

"I used to play . . . Went to Juilliard . . . Then got sidetracked."

He sighed softly.

"Never held a Guarnerius in my hands before. A thrill. An absolute thrill I will never forget."

The inspector slowly, almost reluctantly, put the violin back into the black case.

"I heard you at Carnegie Hall. Mehta was conducting."

"Oh."

The man handed the case back to Shane.

"When's your next concert in New York?"

"I hope to be at Avery Fisher in a few months."

The man's eyes lit up.

"I'll try to be there. But your tickets are hard to get."

"Just come backstage before the concert and I'll see that you have two choice seats."

"Backstage?"

"Yes."

"Will you remember me?"

Shane looked long at him and then smiled sadly.

"I don't think I'll ever forget you."

Then he walked away.

Chapter

32

When he stepped outside into the warm, dark night, a chill feeling came over him, for there was the white Mercedes, gleaming softly, and by it a tall chauffeur in a gray uniform.

His face was hard and impassive.

"Mr. Kent is waiting for you."

Shane went slowly over to the car and looked in.

He saw the lean figure of Kent and next to it that of Elaine Stark.

"Welcome home, Lockwood. Give John the case. He'll put it into the trunk beside your Guarnerius."

Shane stood there, hesitant.

"It's there, Lockwood. I just want you to do me one more favor. A small one."

The chauffeur moved closer to Shane.

"Do as he says."

His right hand lay casually in his jacket pocket.

Shane looked down at it.

"It's a gun," the man said in a low voice.

Shane slowly got into the car and sat down.

Elaine Stark's face was pale.

Her dark eyes looked almost fearfully into his.

Then he heard the car door shut.

Ominously.

Finally.

The car began to move swiftly out of the airport.

"We took a very early morning flight out of Venice," Kent said.

"So you could be here to greet me."

"Exactly."

They rode along in complete silence.

"What is the last favor?" Shane asked quietly.

"The last favor?"

"Yes. The last one."

"It's just a small one."

"You said that."

Kent laughed softly.

"So I did. We have some guests in our Southampton home. I promised them that you would play for them for an hour. And then you can leave. They're eagerly waiting for you. Do you mind?"

Shane didn't answer.

"John will take you to the station and from there you can go on to your home in Princeton. With your Guarnerius."

He paused and then spoke.

"Never to see me again, Lockwood. I promise you that."

Shane turned to look at Elaine Stark.

But she was staring straight ahead of her into the night.

She had not said a word to him.

145

Tell me, Elaine, he wanted to say to her.
Tell me.
Please tell me.
Is he lying to me again?
Is he?
But her lips were pressed together.

Chapter

33

They left the highway and were now riding along a country road. Shane caught glimpses of black water and the white, sandy beaches of the Long Island Sound.

All the time nobody spoke.

And he found himself thinking of Laurie.

The look on her face the last time he saw her.

That wounded look.

He would never see her again.

Never.

"Lockwood."

The car had stopped.

The night about them was vast and silent.

Up on a hillock was a huge white house.

Its lights were on.

A very long gravel driveway led up to the high front doors.

To the left of Shane was the Sound.

Stretching far into the night.

The car door opened and Kent got out.

A sliver of moon had come up in the dark sky and Shane could see his figure as he stood waiting.

"Lockwood."

"You'd better go with him," the chauffeur said.

Elaine Stark turned to Shane.

"Do it," she said.

Their eyes met and then he turned and got out of the car.

"Remember your promise to me, Arthur."

Her words were cold and sharp in the night air.

Kent smiled at her.

"I merely want to speak to him alone. To make sure."

"Your promise," she said and turned away from them.

"Let's go out on the dock where we can talk and not be disturbed," Kent said.

Shane looked at the silent car.

At its white, clean outlines in the dark night.

Then he turned and walked down the tree-lined path and onto the wooden planks of a dock.

Kent closely behind him.

And he knew that the man had the gun in his hand.

"You can stop now," Kent said.

Shane stopped and kept looking past the railing of the dock and out over the stretch of water.

Far, far in the distance he could see the glimmering of two lights.

Somebody is fishing out there.

Content with life.

And free.

He slowly turned and faced the man.

His gray eyes so very cold.

"You never were going to let me go, were you?" Shane said.

The man didn't answer.

His face and hair shone in the darkness.

Richard Cory, Shane thought sardonically.

Then he heard the man's low voice.

"There were times when I thought I would."

"And times? . . ."

The man shook his head.

"When I felt that sooner or later you would talk."

Shane moved a step toward the man.

And he saw the gleam of the gun barrel as it was raised.

"All I want," he said in a fierce voice, "is to get the Guarnerius and to get out of your life. And to get you out of mine. Can't you see that?"

Kent shook his head again.

"I can't. When you hit Mario I knew I couldn't trust you anymore."

"And what are you going to do now? Kill me and dump me into the Sound. Never to be found again?"

"I'm afraid that is your destiny, Lockwood."

"Then do it."

Kent slowly raised the gun and it was then that Shane heard the shot and saw the man stagger back and then fall heavily to the floor of the dock.

He lay flat, his eyes staring up, a bullet hole in his forehead.

The blood streaming from it.

Shane looked up and saw Elaine Stark.

Her face was white and drawn.

Her dark, brooding eyes staring at him.

Then she spoke in a low and dull voice.

149

"He promised me that he would let you go. Promised me."

Shane leaned back against the railing of the dock.

His hands trembling violently.

Then he heard the gun drop and clatter on the wood.

Her voice came through to him.

"It's over, Shane. Over."

She began to sway and he went to her and put his arms about her.

"Elaine," he said.

Then he heard her speak.

"Over. My life is over. I'll go back to Venice and never leave it again."

He slowly let her go.

She stood there looking long at him.

"I'll see that the tiara is returned to the museum. I've come to hate it. The tiara really belongs to Laurie Guiccioli. You know that, don't you?"

He didn't speak.

"John will take you to the station. Go home, Shane. Go home."

He turned for one last look at her, and then he left the dock.

Chapter

34

He had walked all the way from Carnegie Hall to Washington Square. The snow was falling and his hair was white with its flakes.

It was evening and the light was fading.

The concert had been a great success.

But within his heart he knew that it wasn't.

Something was missing.

Something would always be missing.

He walked through the park, past Garibaldi's statue, when he saw her.

She was sitting alone on a bench just staring at the snow.

He went over and silently sat down by her.

She looked up at him but didn't move.

"Laurie," he said.

"Please leave."

"No."

"There is someone else. I've gotten over you."

"I haven't. I've been looking for you."

"We were going too fast, you said. Why look for me?"

"I can explain."

"I don't want to hear it."

Her voice broke.

"Laurie."

She suddenly rose and started walking away from him.

"Laurie. Laurie Guiccioli, I love you and will always love you."

She stopped and turned to him.

Then he slowly went up to her and took her into his arms.

She began to cry softly.

The snow came down upon them.

Gently.

So very gently.

JAY BENNETT

THE HOODED MAN
Cory felt his life was over when his best friend, Fred, was killed while they were playing a fraternity prank. Ever since the accident, Cory has been stalked by a mysterious hooded figure who blames Cory and seeks revenge. And soon it may be Cory's turn to die.

SING ME A DEATH SONG
Marian Feldon is to be executed for the murder of her lover, and the only person who believes her to be innocent is her teenage son, Jason. With only days to go, Jason learns a secret at the bedside of a dying stranger that could save his mother if it doesn't kill him first!